Crossing the Line

A threat to unethical Politicians, Bureaucrats and cheap Educationists

Aabhas K Maldahiyar

Publisher : **Diamond Pocket Books (P) Ltd.**
X-30, Okhla Industrial Area, Phase-II
New Delhi-110020
Phone : 011-40712200
E-mail : sales@dpb.in
Website : www.diamondbook.in

Crossing the Line
By : Aabhas K Maldahiyar

Dedicated to all who dare to raise voice against ills of the system!

Acknowledgement

This book is indeed an episode from the chronicle of Great Combat against the decaying acerbic system and a story of such credibility always has a large populace threading the same. I'm extremely grateful to Prof. Sanjadhi Chatterjee who significantly plays the role of "Krishna" in this fight and is always there with fantabulous suggestions and denigration whenever needed.

I'm in deep debt to my Mother for the precious time she imparted to make me learn the basics in language of scripting which has finally helped me to at-least bring up the story. Also a bouquet of thanks is a must for my Grandmother, whose storytelling skill has helped me give a try for few. My intense fume of gratitude goes to my Father whose principles have found deep roots within me. I'm also thankful to Achal Maldahiyar, Mukesh Sinha (Uncles), Rigvendra Aayush, Siddharth Sourabh, Kunal Sinha (Brothers) all the sisters and rest whole family members who ever helped me at their best.

I'm also extremely thankful to my Alma Matters' family, Piloo Mody College of Architecture and D.A.V. Public School, Hazaribagh for training me the best as the one.

There is no way, the damsel, and queen of my thoughts, Tejal Pardhy cannot be thanked. I'm very thankful to her for continuously rousing me walk ahead with the notion to bring best for the globe.

I'm very obliged to Prof. Uday Gadkari, Prof. Abhay Purohit, Prof. Milind Gujarkar and whole IDEAS family who encourage me in taking up pen despite hectic working calendar. But there are few from this family who need special mentions, Ar. Amit Shelke for assisting me in designing cover page, Prof. Mankar, for regularly inflaming my thoughts and structuring them with proper reinforcement. I'm also thankful to buddies at IDEAS, Harshal Sir, Devendra Sir and Manoj Sir who helped me maintain my tempo to write. I'm enormously gratified to all my dear students at IDEAS who have actually been best teachers of my life.

There are large bulk of people whom I have never met but they have been an essential contributor for the book you are holding, lots of gratitude goes to Himani Goyal and Abhilash Veeru Ruhela for the candid review of "Restart" (my first book), which has helped me improvise many times in my writing skills. I'm extremely thankful to all the readers of same who this way or other encouraged me to pen down the next. I'm very thankful to Vishal Anand who has been regularly floating me with abundant of suggestions and critical appraisals throughout the progress of manifesto.

Also vote of thanks goes to Vaibhav Kaushal, my school mate who helped me generate ideas for promotional video along with his younger brother, Gyandeep (Author of "The TEEN").

There is no way I can ignore few people's concern, who are no less than gems. Special token of thanks goes to Vinod Pardhi, Preeti Singh ma'am, Nitin Vinay Khare and Prashant Gandhi who regularly kept suggesting me whenever needed.

Last but not the least, a heartiest thanks also goes to Mr.Narendra Verma; Chairman, Diamond Pocket Books and the entire team of Diamond Pocket Books for giving me part of their esteemed family.

–Aabhas K Maldahiyar
aabhasinpmca@gmail.com

Prologue

He keeps racing for his life through the unknown woods of Keonjhar, Orissa. His feet were tangling; he escapes on numerous occasions before finally being crashed into a large tree. He could sniff earth dusts to soon get blemished into the state of unconsciousness that almost meant a death to him, as pellet was pierced into his thigh, and the chemical was sure to show its honesty. The party time for Ghost-rider appeared too close and approaching.

However, fortune is always written to be an un-anticipated verb for natural beings. It proves its worth yet again. He is fortuned to fall at the hand of other troubles post to meet with king of heaven or hell.

He feels some twinge in whole body and finds it uphill to push up visionary shutters, but when it opens, things around seems feathered and faded. Although gradually the objects around were turning lucid and prominent. Shuddery aghast arrives as soon as the photons from optical organ reflects back to portray the existents, he seems anonymous habitant to the inside's surrounding. So far taught and studied vernacularism of built spaces was in front of him.

A person appears to be standing near the orifice of built set up; again anonymity was a sure expression knowing the manifestation he was in. The person was wearing military attire, hanging a long barrel gun to a side. He was dark in complexion and tall in height; just few inches less to a lintel while his long bushy moustache almost made curve to meet side burns, at the same time a scarce on his face yelled to describe his aggression and fierce attitude.

"Be tucked in there. You are under our custody," he tells in a high alarming tone pointing through his hands. Adi jabs back to the rope cot. The man keeping an eye on him peeps outside and whistles making some hand postures. Soon just after a gap of fraction of minute, three more men come in. They wore almost similar dressing as that of the first person. One of those three, walking in the middle of two, didn't carry a big barreled gun, though a pistol was stuck to his waist. He was very tall and very fair in complexion while solidity reflected from his countenance and he seemed to be the leader of all.

One thing was common among all, the scares and cut marks on their faces along with the outfit they wore.

"Who are you?" asks the leader in bold, manly and heavy voice. He emerged to be a strong man and frightening too.

Nothing much runs through his brain, he was not sure for what to speak. He blabbers while speaking, "I'm Adi…" he didn't complete, but soon replied, "Adiraj Shrivastava. I teach in a private primary school."

"Hmm…how did you come in our vicinity?" asks the leader, again using his imposing voice.

"Some unknown people were trying to kill me; I tried to run away in order to save my life, and I don't know how I made it into your den," he replies. He seems to be little worried as his voice was stammering.

"Kill you? But why? Don't even dare to speak lies. We are very dangerous people, playing with life is fun to us."

Traces of sweat appear on his face while leader keeps throttling his nerves. Soon they disperse away leaving him all alone lying within the mud built set up. There was a sole opening, from where beam of light was coming in; its reddish hue clearly demarked the day turning off, as the different chorus of chirpings were deeply heard, also signifying them being stationed in deep woods. His brain makes an alarm by then, he had concludes-*he is fallen at the hands of Naxalites.* He tries to stand on his feet, but the wound on thigh didn't let him do so..

Horror seemed penetrating deep into his heart, his phone and other belongings were missing and those missed goods were indeed clue to 'The Identity'. The hand of doubt pointed it on his captor, but if at all, they might have killed him by then. He was not certain.

It was never easy due to let the time pass by for hostile urgency running around. He goes till the low heighted door kind of opening of the hut where he was captivated in, while walking down, little pain occurred, following which his expressions turn squashy. It was all very dark around, the humming sound of insects and barks of jackals and wolfs were breaching the real silence ramming through. Few beams of light were visible from various habitat pockets around. At a mere distance of about century of feet, saffron flames kissed the black violet sky. The February cloud, wore indigo outline, which was glittering to full.

Soon, few men again appear; none of them were those whom he saw earlier. Same attire reflects there uniformity.

"How are you feeling now? Hopefully your wound is recovering well enough," says one of those unknowns while hinting others to leave.

"Hmm…I'm recovering well, though little pining pain still remains," he responds.

"Sit down there," That man orders and they both sit down on the cot, "I have to tell something very important to you."

"Yeah, tell me…I'm listening," Adi says with a node.

That man again gets up and peeps around as if to make sure, no one is around. A kind of drama seems to be running in front of Adi. Suddenly, Adi's eyes spread wide to witness the happenings to be followed soon. That man unfolds a pouch and opens it to take out his missing chattels, the mobile phone and wallet.

"Oh shit! I never noticed, they went missing and how did you find them?" Adi asks in a shudder, scrambling worry for some reasonable occurrence fishes him.

1. The Arrival

The passion and craze to touch the motherland soil after a year was aggressively impatient. It had been long when I smelt the earthy cozy smell; last it was during the monsoon, a couple of years back from then. I was travelling back to the great peninsula. Cock-tailed emotions were bursting through my nerves, throat lump was persuading to and fro in a pace insisting *around* about my nervousness.

I sat resting alongside to the window, through that I never peeped; because even till then the phobia of 'Z' remained in me. The past twenty-five months had been striking, precious for the impending days to come by. The memories of Prof. Shubhrat and his revolutionary attire was still fresh blazing in me. Nevertheless, the return was shaped on the glider of Journalist.

I kept thinking about the memories of the past, in the meanwhile saccharine voice came up, "Good Evening Ladies and Gentlemen! We will be landing at Indira Gandhi InterNational Airport, New Delhi within next ten minutes. All of you are requested to put on your seat belts. Hope you had an awesome journey. Thank you!" The long awaited alarming sentences.

Plane dashed through the runway, my beats were multiplying with summing of time. It was an un-anticipated expression; I had never thought that heart would be so profound while accomplishing the quest to be, where I was, through my major past. *Aryavarta* had been calling me since I had my stern faced to her.

I got out of the airport; haste and enthusiasm were flowing in the forms of sweat. I never cared to wipe them off, indeed it was an appreciative cloak gifted by Tropicana. I had been deprived of this heat for long, never this sweat peaked me during the last quarter century of past months; and there it was kissing and romancing with me high in the erotic, Delhi winds of July.

The white *khadi* shirt had turned grey beneath arms and same overlay had appeared at back too, as it was embraced tight with my back and abdomen. I hired a taxi to Lajpat Nagar; I had planned this surprise for Rizwan a month ago.

I cared enough so as to assure that my schedule was never detailed to him; I had only shared my eagerness and willingness to return India soon.

***

"Brother, please hold on for a while," I instructed the driver.

I got down. "Please, do it soon sir," The driver urged. I replied with a node coated with smile and I went ahead to the grocery shop.

"Please give me a water bottle," I pleaded the plump shopkeeper wearing a smile.

"Here it is…twenty rupees," he said. The witty smile unknowingly spoke a lot, indeed, it had to, and also a journalist was upfront. Moreover, the initial tempo of any new journey is always sparkly with little hue of blemishes. I scanned the bottle, and I was shocked to see guy charging supplementary six bucks.

"Brother, the MRP is something six bucks less than what you are charging. This is off beam," I emphasized.

"This is the way it happens. Nothing new!" agitation glittered on his face. I paid him and left. Some bug had found existence in me; it was the rarer of occasions when I purchased a packaged drinking water.

I reached to the apartment where Rizwan stayed. I rang the bell long enough to disturb the sweetest beauty of sleep yanking Mr. Architect. Door opened in a while. There stood green fellow, heaved with the sleep. The sap green vests and widened aloe shaded tracks justified him being an employee of Arcop, The Green Architects.

"Fucker, couldn't you inform once before arriving?" He told, punching supple at my super flat belly. After the time he had let me in, we shared lots and lots of missed gears from when +91 got detached from me. The time seemed to be tricking in a bit too fast, as none of us wanted to spare each other's company. He later even abused me for meeting him for only sparse duration, but I was bound.

***

The journey to Ranchi started that evening, in a slipper coach of 'Jharkhand Express'. This was happening after largely lingered moments. The excitement to feel the departed times of early twenties was high on me. The youth generation of then must have found me crazy, travelling in Non-AC compartment. However, been there beyond the borders, and the studies of reporting and journalism had made me realize well the connotation of 'We the people'.

I often feel pity on Hippocratic Attitude of youth, it's hampering our system most.

I sat graphing upper and lower part nearing right angle, watching through the window, the breeze kept flapping my nose. My gaze remained passing through the pages of 'Alchemist' -the book Prof. Shubhrat had found to change his perception long back during his post graduation and the celebratory factor remained, as he was one of those who provoked me to restart after the passive death phase amid my college days.

The sweet mechanical voice continued making its charisma, being marked because of the available fenestrations. The music was on; the monotony of tenor was very adorable and perceptible. It had been so anonymous to me since so many yesterdays.

I walked down through the bogie to maintain proper plasma flow in my nerves. Soon delight and acute contentment thronged me, the long past fantasy stood affirm upfront. She appeared as a campus teen ornamented in the lap of a guy. Both stayed on side lower berth. The micro surrounding lunar eclipse remained as visual cone found 'Rebel' in between. 'Smile' became necessary there in a while, as the book of mine was being read and I was not noticed so far as the scripter of the one.

I wanted to reach in the hearts of youth, it never happened initially but it seemed the sparkles had begun glooming. I wished to explain, "It's me-*The author* of what you are reading", but never did so. I walked ahead. I put the ear chords and pressed the music button in phone and stood leaning to the door.

The sky had turned grey, twinkles were getting prominent,

and the satellite remained behind the curtain. The waft kept puffing my face. The amount of satisfaction was breaching its point of yield. As closer I was getting, sickness was crawling more and more.

The steel wheel, the lever, the conveyer belt went enchanting the mechanical sound while doziness kept arriving. I got back to the berth; the clock read 9:30 pm by then. Sleep clutched me, and I lied on blue cushion carefree in the National carrier.

Vibrations appeared in my jeans pocket while sweet tweets broke my sleep. I opened eyes to see bright day. Glare was incident on forehead. Tiredness had a toll on me. I stretched my arms upwards and smiled wide in myself to greet back Mr. Sun. I sat up. Other passengers were already very active fulfilling basic train journey morning rituals, busy making sip of tea and coffee, few stood queued for the rest areas.

"When will we reach the final station?" I asked the TTE.

"By around noon," he replied. Delight reached beyond throat. I dashed below to drag my large bag out. I took out tooth brush, paste and a face wash.

After freshening and being partially cleaned, I purchased a *kulhad* of tea. *Kulhads* are special clay utensils that were primarily used in India till few years post to autonomy. I ever found food cooked in clay utensils very scrumptious and was very blissful to get the special tea after so long.

"Hello sir!" appeared a feminine accent. I looked up, and greeted with a node and smile.

"Sir, if I'm not wrong, you are Ar.Aditya, The Author of 'Rebel'?" She said with a wide smile of delight, happiness and excitement.

"Yes, I'm Aditya Sinha," I replied, "The author of 'Rebel'," a triumphed smile gloomed on my face.

"Oh, really! What a lovely unforeseen surprise sir! It is really implausible. I just read your book last night," she said hurriedly.

"Oh... That's great! How did you find it?" I asked, hiding all the erupting emotions within.

"Sir, the story is simply remarkable. This changed my perception overnight. You are just wonderful!" She kept airing me with lots and lots of praises.

I listened to her happily. But obviously, this was one of the best moments an author keeps waiting for. Talking to her, I had found-she was a student of Biotechnology at Birla Institute of Technology, Ranchi. She was impressed to know, that I returned India after perusing *Masters in Journalism* from Michigan University. She also took my signature and message on the book. We kept chatting until our destination: the final station arrived. Both of us greeted each other and left. It was from her that I came to know about the great popularity 'Rebel' found after I left India.

***

The station was still the same. Development was sparse enough to make its presence negligible. Thirteen years had passed by when Jharkhand was separated from Bihar, but pathetically, bloody politicians never bothered to think about its progress. The partition of Bihar had lots of hope incased, but the consequences came inversely proportional to the expectations.

The phone rang with vibration. I realized my mistake to see the call from Aparajita. I never rang home since boarding the train.

"Brother, where are you? By when are you reaching here?" Aparajita asked on phone.

"Oops! Sorry! I could not call due to low battery," I replied overlapping the mistake committed, "I have reached station, and will be reaching Home within some time." I disconnected the phone after conversing for some five minutes.

I left to bus stand hiring an auto rickshaw, boarded a bus from there and finally I was a duo and half hours due to reach my home.

The journey in the bus drove me back to the era of past. The events were nearly analogous to how I used to get back home during vacations. The reminiscences were yet very unsullied and juvenile. I kept peeping roadside and the surroundings visible from the bus. Apartment and townships had covered all the empty spaces of the past. The city seemed jam-packed. Greeneries were missing, though few new plantations were visible.

Mother Nature had faced so much of set back at the cost of 'Development', what her offsprings call. The Architect,

Journalist was dying to contribute best at force while the humane in me was crying in the pain of superficial development.

It was 7:45 pm when the bus dropped me at the bus stand of Hazaribagh.

The zone was dark, though natural violet shade was still able to illuminate little till before turning black. Little lights flashed in few shops while many were still Kerosene lit. The scene upfront portrayed the backwardness my hometown faced. In the era of twenty-first century, electricity is still a matter of concern; this was a sign of extreme pessimism. I felt an urge to cover loads and loads of homework to be completed. Manual rickshaw seemed still in operation, as they hung around at various corners, though they all bundled out whenever a bus came in. Again only thing that could come up at the name of development was loss in the number of trees.

I had heard from so many natives, "Hazaribagh has advanced a lot in the field of education. Now we have Dental/Medical and Engineering colleges here. There are so many preparatory coaching institutes as well, those fulfil students' dream to become Engineer or Doctor."

Both elders and students often forget that their dream might befall on either side for this Nation; they can be boon or even the nightmare.

Finally, I took a manual rickshaw, after being unable to find any auto nearby. I would have preferred walking along the remaining 4 KMs but the weight of the sack on my back never permitted, and even I never felt practice of manual rickshaws human in nature.

As I traversed through the recognizable roads, the number of hoardings for Coaching Institutes and Education Consultancies kept on increasing. It was never the same as two years back.

As I crossed Wales cricket ground of St.Columbas College, the moments of yesterdays came in again. It was the same ground where my bouncer had coasted my coach a couple of teeth. Wonderful were the days. Ah! ...how pleasant it would have been if golden days lingered till we got bored out of them. Unfortunately, we can't play game on the board named 'Time' instead it plays out on us.

It was twenty minutes of rigorous paddling by the brave rickshaw-puller, after which I reached 'Nath Cottage-My home'. I paid him a hundred bucks, he was more than delighted. He wanted to return few change, but I denied saying, "Brother, you work a lot. Extreme labor is involved and you deserve a lot more. Take care of your health too." He left giving me lots of blessings.

I was happy from within; he went more than happy leaving from my doorstep. I don't go to temples, but helping these poor chaps and dragging their problems away is the best practice for me as a human being.

❑

2. Home after long

"*Arre, Brother!* You have come…yeah…" Atriz came running at the entrance gate. The whole family was sitting in the lawn trying to fight back the extreme summer. Thank god! Light was glooming and electricity was present. I greeted all elders by bending and touching their feet. All were delighted to feel my presence after a long interval. Mummy, Papa, the Uncles and Aunts, Granny, Aparajita, Aditi, Atriz all expressed the bundles of happiness.

We chit chatted whole night after the dinner, as I stood at the centre showing small gifts brought for all. They heard whole-heartedly, my experience at the university abroad.

***

"I will sleep on the terrace, I have not felt these unsullied air and autonomy since long," I told mother as she asked me to sleep watching at the diminishing time.

"No ways! You will fall ill. The temperature will be quite low later in the night," she said but finally agreed as I insisted long.

It was after so many pasts that I was able to feel the sovereignty and novelty in the slumber. It was a sound sleep before when I could feel something sharp hitting on my head. I woke up in a jerk and was surprised to find a crow sitting on my head. He just flew away reacting to my retort. The day was already bright yellow by then. The rays were now thorny and uttering hard from southeast.

As a daily morning custom, I peeped through the cell phone, there were three missed call and a text message. I unlocked it to find-*were r u? I tried calng, bt u nvr pickd.swt dreams.Gudnite.cal wen u free*, a text message from Trisha.

I called her back, “Where had you been? I tried calling you so many times,” voice of Trisha appeared, “You always used to receive calls, even when you were in the US. This is appalling.”

“I’m sorry dear, exhaustion didn’t let me react. Indeed, I have travelled through the continents. I had sent you a facebook message earlier the time I landed in India, but it seems you didn’t receive it,” I tried to convey and persuade.

I talked with her for some times, in the meanwhile I heard Mummy coming upstairs and even the glare was getting sharper. I kept the phone saying, “Ok, dear. Mummy is coming, will call you up very soon. Take care. Bye!”

“I thought, you are still sleeping, so just came to wake you up,” Mummy told as she reached on the terrace.

“No, Mom, I’m not that lazy anymore,” I said hugging Mom from behind.

“Ok, no need to grease me. Go and get organized soon, breakfast is ready. All are waiting for you,” she said and left.

I rushed to the lavatory on the terrace. I really needed to be fast, all were to go out for their respective jobs. Thinking about job, the bubbles had started playing in my tummy. I kept thinking positioned on WC: indeed *it’s a think tank for we technocrats, since the times of Archimedes and many more*.

I was offered a job, in a MNC at Singapore as an Architect Journalist. But some other accentuation nodes were yanking me strong. Newton’s laws are psychologically and sociologically true too, it was proving its worth on these dimensions and I was able to feel it.

It was a pleasant feeling being showered by the indigenous priceless pearls of life. I wished to stay longer under it, but the time was tricking fast for other family fellows who had been waiting for me to have breakfast.

The scenario of the family and their perspective towards me seemed highly changed; it was never the same till my graduation and prior. I was a worthless pebble and even bit similar to any eclipse. Whatever the past may be, it’s always best to chuck them all and look forward for a brighter tomorrow with the sense of togetherness. I was also happy; as after so long kin was dining together. The ovens and utensils were not one, cracks had occurred within the Sinha family. But again, the separation got diminished subsequent to my arrival.

Keeping thoughts aside, I was ready soon. The whole family had breakfast jointly, forth to that all departed for their respective works.

***

It was in the noon, when I was talking with Aparajita about her studies. She was at home, as her summer vacations were on till next two days.

"Yes brother, Prof. has asked us to pay money in order to get passing grades in engineering drawing," she complained me about one of her professors. I felt like laughing and being exasperated as well, I was astounded.

This is a real sorry state of our Education System. What can one expect from other class of society if 'Teachers-The society makers' themselves breath the dignity and make the divine pond dirty.

"Ok, I'll talk to your Director. This is a serious concern and I cannot take hold of it," I said, taking agitation to full.

"Moreover, brother, my mates call me a fool. They say, 'Why do you want to add complexity if marks are falling to your pocket this easily'," she added further.

I replied with a smile, "you are not a fool, they are the fools. We can't perceive or project our future in the haze of momentary luxury and happiness. Same is happening with your batch-mates."

I promised and assured of meeting her Director very soon. Hearing about grey patches in Education- System was not new to me. I have been able to feel it since matriculation. World seems so fraud and hypocrite after that. They teach us subject called moral education, but I wished if they contained even a partial of it in real life. This song seems so very much truthful.

"Bachche man ke sachche,
Sare jag ki ankh ke tare.
Yeh who nanhein fool hain jo,
Bhagwan ko lagte pyare.
Khud ruthein khud man jayein,
Phir humjoli ban jayein.
Jhagda jinke sath karein,

Agle hi pal phir baat karein.
Jyon jyon inki umar badhe,
Man par jhooth ka mail chadhe.
Krodh badhe nafrat ghere,
Lalach ki aadat ghere.
Inka bholapan achcha hai,
Sabki rah sudharein.
Bachche man ke sachche,
Sare jag ki ankh ke tare."

However, kids seem to get matured sooner now days. Reasons might be many for this. The fast learning and adapting skill might be one of those. But it's real unfortunate, they use to learn what they should never, but they hardly learn what they should. *The Abhimanyus of today*!

***

The day went past rapidly fast. Night arrived very soon. The anxiety of getting a job was digging my pulse hard. I didn't had, the courage to tell parents and family about the offer I had declined. I had been waiting for response from Chandrakant sir. He was the principal of my college during my graduation. Now, he owned an Architecture School partnered with few other Architects. I was looking for my chance to get a professor's seat there. Wearing father's shoes has been a trend in Indian society since long, and teaching to me seemed noblest profession of all although recent years showed me the corrupt pictures of same as well, but my affinity for troubles needed me there as well.

I put laptop on, placed it on thighs while lying supported to three thick pillows. I logged in to Gmail and Yahoo mail. Inbox in Google showed three new arrivals, while there were fifteen offline messages from Trisha in Yahoo. I made a call to her while opening inbox, there was an email from Chandrakant sir's college, it was subjected- *Appointment letter*: a hint for Nagpur's call.

Further Trisha had picked the phone, "Hi dear! You are so bad, you are calling after so long." She quenched.

"Yes dear, I'm very sorry for that. I had been very busy for the whole day. You know it very well, how family would be feeling after watching their guy returned after twenty five months. In the meanwhile, I have very good news for you," I convinced.

"Oh! Good news... You are coming to Nagpur." She declared.

"Yeah, just in a week. And, finally we are going to meet," saying this I added to her delight. We conversed for around an hour before landing to the wonderland.

I was shrinking to the black hole. The gravity was bit too strong. Many times, I thought about fate and destiny. But, finally I have turned rationalist. Destiny is what we dream for, and destiny has to be reached. It befalls contrary to what we normally feel that: destiny makes thing happen.

Black hole is indeed very baffling for many as a noun; it is also the final attainment of a star and also the sign of death.

This was working great for me, passion and adore was calling me.

Indeed, whatever we wish is actually like a treasure and our will to get it is the deed of its hunt.

❑

3. The new journey

The looming week flew very swift and brisk. I could not make to so many promises, yet again I promised to cover them up in next round trip.

Yeah, it is true, they loved me then, rather power was making them swirl body for the never thought turns and twists. My Dad was a proud man now, I was set to begin an endeavor, that too wearing his shoes. I was to join an Architecture School as Assistant Professor and pack-up happened very soon.

***

It was a composite journey of bus and train, summing to a travel time of seventeen hours. I reached there at seven in the morning. I had planned to stay in a hotel, till college provided me with proper lodging.

I called up Chandrakant Sir, to make the intimation of my arrival. He was very delighted to find me arrived, he further crossed my idea to stay in a hotel. He instructed me to stay at his abode till proper arrangements were made. There was no point flying bubbles of formality, I stuck to his sayings. However, I reached to his beautifully designed mansion. I greeted him by touching his feet, he loaded me with lots of benedictions, and his vision seemed overwhelmed.

He showed me the guesthouse. I shifted my baggage there. He prepared breakfast in a brisk and it was really a pleasure. Sir was known for his culinary skills, we, all his students of PMCA used to enjoy his hand made treats very often.

Next morning, we left to the college together in his car for my 'interview and joining'.

It all went smooth and splendid. The Principal put few very interesting and amazing questions to me, as "Why did you pursue post graduation in 'Journalism', a totally drastic different stream?"

"For a small, yet urgent reason–I dreamt of correcting 'System –as a whole', and the best way to do so is to learn it. Journalism indeed is one of the best preachers. Architecture taught me a lot as well; after all, it is Societal Engineering. Now, I wish to get into the Education System: the backbone of all," I explained.

"Will you please expound more about your sudden incliNation towards teaching; or Education System: as you say?" asked The Principal Sir.

"Yes sir, sure. I have seen my Father serve as Professor ever since my dawn. He taught me the essence of a teacher for the society; I too grew up with passion for this noble social profession. The day, I entered Architecture School, the problems and tribulations started being visible and known. Gradually, my many pals and I suffered at the hands of cupid brutality of python. I went to a grey phase in middle; pen came out as the best help then. I restarted my life there at the school by penning down 'Rebel': my debut novel, it holds the color of revolution and rage against the evils of Education System. I was all determined to quit 'Architecture' and start a new career in the stream of literature and reporting, but my mentor and very much a friend Prof. Shubhrat said, 'Don't quit, otherwise people will claim, this happened as a consequence of your disgrace for stream. You have analyzed problems well, now; it's your responsibility to show the solutions as well'." I explained him deeply.

"Ok. That is good, but how do you see the things ahead. I mean–Will your approach towards teaching in a different and revolutionary fashion?" Another one came by The Boss.

"Yes sir, my attempt will be lying somewhere close to this. I will try my best to bring sustainable bridge between practicality and academics. Normally professors, insist academics and practical field are totally different ball game comparatively. Because of this barbaric statements, pupil never take academics seriously, instead good academics only means high magnitude grades and steps towards a first class degree. When a bridge will fall, we will never look at those fantastic pieces of paper but a solution would be needed, which is never bookish, instead it is only and only aptitude based. I'm searching for clues to these underlying queries," I said.

The ideas were pretty crude and raw, but the dream was soaring high.

The lines by Paulo Coelho are most inspiring and workable for me: "When you want something, the entire universe conspires in helping you to achieve it."

Principal Sir was contented with my answers. All the Directors were happy to see me as a part of their college family. After the interview session, Chandrakant sir spared his precious time to introduce me with all the faculties. I was able to sense the climate of freedom for both the students and the instructors.

The journey had begun at a correct initial juncture, I thought.

***

Evening had loaded me with lots of argues to celebrate. I was on debut date with Adorable. Trisha and I sat opposite at the couches of CCD, for first few moments our eyes kept fluttering without much action by the lips, we remained numb partially bent with elbow pressed on table and palms supported jaws. Her divine beauty was forcing my medulla to pluck in a hug, and the pinkish coffee shade of espresso bar was further turning to be catalyst. The pouring ivory luminal along with the contrasting dark eve outside was helping me perceive my Damsel Lady even more striking. Ah...her black long skirt with befallen curly hair, the full lips of her were erupting the ever sweet wine for me, the vivid pelt and the eyes placed amid sweet partially risen nose off-beating geometry of fish altogether kept mesmerizing me for long.

I had never seen her before, earlier it was all in the stationary pictures on screen and quite often in video chats of Skype. Amazingly incredible, it may seem to lots, but yes, I met my better half through a social network.

We both were happy, as the dreams were coming true.

Happiness indeed is the reaction busted out of 'Attraction reached', and, then the point of accentuation becomes our chattels.

"Are you happy now?" She asked.

"Yeah, I'm super delighted. After long, it seems, things are working the way I wanted. Dreams are being turned into destiny, and when it happens, complexity diverge," I said, "but, you know, we humans are perfectly shaped. With the 'greed' to add on, we can achieve distant of things. *Only, 'greed' is ought to be honest and non materialistic*."

"True, I'm really lucky to have one like you as my companion. I can learn bundles and be more inspired to dream and achieve, through my life," she said, interlocking her fingers with mine. Current ran through my nerves, the first commotion is always something beyond definite. For a while, I was taken aback by the smooth draftiness of beauty.

Her face wore an adorable smile. Her beautiful deep eyes, hinted me for her acceptance and assent.

We both left from there by around three hours before mid of the night. She planted a goodnight kiss, on my right wrist. Its maiden sense benched me high.

She blushed little with a smile and faded away driving her Scooty. The touch of her lips had brought an unknown aroma. I kissed back there on my wrist, closing the eye, marveling into the dreamland. Soon, I was into the senses realizing for the falling time. I hired an auto-rickshaw to the home of Chandrakant Sir.

Sir was already at the home, when I reached. He was watching a news channel. It was showing the coverage on newly inserted amendment in the Education System. Human Resource Minister, Sachin Dev was on live; explaining it. "See, the grading system will erase burden of the kids. In the absence of much load and pressure, they will be able to learn the things well. Even the eradication of board examinations during matriculation and higher secondary standards will grow them more innovative."

"Bloody fool," sir didn't notice, I blabbered and moved to the guest house.

I still remember the turnover in my career. His introduced pattern of IIT-JEE had ruined so many things.

The IITs have truly fallen short of anticipated level, and the output is not the same as their past alumni are. The best premiere institute of Science and Engineering starves for marvelous preachers and also the students of now lack in the fervor for innovation.

Many professional schools of India majorly including, IITs,

NITs; IIMs are suffering by the bug of brain drain and stream change. The song of placement and wealth accumulation is catering there precious years being three, four or five. Engineers prefer serving social networking web sites as there hoists, financial sectors as business analysts; they also accept the classy posts offered by banks, while those in the field of business have started creating cheap business opportunities.

It really makes me feel pity thinking: *The ought to be National infrastructure builders are busy building the greenery in their bank accounts, working hard on making family future bight, brighter, brightest.*

But, why still HRD doesn't wish to control this paradigm shift instead of trying to make more like them? Our country is suffering, still this situation can't be kept being hilarious as its continuing.

"Come, let's have dinner," sir broke the ride of my mind. I was back to the real world in a shudder.

"Yeah…yes sir, coming!" I replied; initial stammer made him stare at me for a while. I smiled and proceeded. We had a great dinner that night, long after I got this opportunity. We had some light talks during dinner, I shared with him my experience of thesis and the life spent at Michigan University. He was very happy to hear my views about the system. He cherished my reverie, to replace this system.

He told at last, "Aditya, things are not that uncomplicated in actuality. The system has already taken the monster form. It is true, we need to do something soon on priority, but question remains. How?" Sir said and left for the doze greeting me a Good-Night. I reciprocated and went to sleep as well.

***

Sir's question had filled me with anxiety. Whole night dreams kept cluttering me in cocktailed form, beauty of Trisha, her commotion and the taunts of system, though they were not very clear and visible in the dreamy eyes, as tiredness was sure to give its reflexes. Just the night had to pass, and it did.

❑

4. Swift drive

I was assigned to teach 'Design' and 'Acoustics'. Very rapidly a bonding was developed between students and me. They were now coming up as my follower. My experiments in the system were coming worthy and fruitful to begin with.

I was trying the paramount to deliver all, which I felt *missed*, during my college life. At the same moment, I kept writing for few journals. My articles had also started finding a place in many English and Hindi dailies. Journalism and teaching 'Architecture' kept racing in chorus with the common goal 'to rectify'.

A new venture had begun as well; I had started practicing 'Architecture', the designs proposed by me were apposite to the need and context.

***

It was again a push from Prof. Shubhrat that I started practicing Architecture. He had come to Nagpur-*his hometown*, in a vacation. We were chitchatting and discussing being seated in a bar. This breed of long-term debate on some serious topic was carrying on after a very protracted time gap.

Sir said, "Adi, all is good, it will be better and might be the best if you start practicing. You are making your best to cover the differences at the level of academics, apply the same *mantra* here too. Practice 'Architecture' the way it should be like, let the lost adjective prevail." The words sufficiently contained lots of boost and motivations with promises to make me run on the smoky path.

I kept thoughtful silence for few seconds, while Prof. took another sip of rum, biting cucumber partly. Then I said, 'Sir, you are right! Architects don't practice the noble profession in the way it should have been. They have been violating principles and ethics since long. They know well how to blast students for their mistakes, but they keep on breaching and committing the mistakes, rather the blunders. I witnessed an incidence just few days back."

"What was that?" Sir asked me inquisitively wearing a frown.

I started narrating, "I was out to a neighbor Architecture School along with my students to attend an Architectural occurrence. A very renowned Architect presented his works to the audience, he was the same person, who had once fired Gajyendra for his design of Vertical Farming, claiming design to be old and nothing new had been done. He had also criticized him for the mistakes at structural level. The words of Mr. Architect contained lots of confrontation, belligerence that had left Gajyendra morally behind, full of disgrace and scattered with the odor of daunt. It had happened while he was displaying his works in NIASA Best Thesis Awards. The real mockery happened in front of me when Architect sir, made the moments lighter, giggling at the trembling architectural mistakes he committed. Then, I just wanted to say, 'Bloody..., he did it in the college academics sheets, for that you penalized him dragging away his honor. Who will penalize you for the mistakes committed practically, which is bringing bundles of problem to the users'?"

"Yes, I remember that session of Gajyendra. This is a sad fact, what we teach is never executed. Two reasons lies, first is that; syllabus is hardly refined with the pace of shifting time while the second is, they are bit too ethical for the professionals, guardians and even the teachers to trail," he said.

"Then sir, some day everything will cave into pieces. Saturation is an un-avoidable state. In the quest to feed stomach of dishonest greed and the fear to walk on longer ways, we have left mother earth covered with the probability of nearing yield." I said; fear was loaded in my talk.

"The concern is not only about 'Architecture', even all additional professions including 'Medical', 'Teaching' and many others have also fallen prey to this. The whole system needs a fanatical homework," Prof. tried to make me understand.

His views were very correct, he too wanted to fetch lots of revolution, he attempted many times, but unfortunately, the ties of family and professional accountability never let him spread wings wider.

This conversation was beginning for outputs from a highly charged medulla. My perception started finding change at a brisk pace. I never thought if groundwork was optimum to resist the rumbling but I accepted it easily.

***

Trisha had turned out to be an urgent part of my life by then; the dependency on her had grown to max. Frequency of the phone calls had increased, and we had started meeting very often.

I was also guiding her for the graduation thesis. On my suggestion, she did a thesis on: 'An ideal By-Law'. This topic was so virgin and anti system that it was not fitting in the eyes of her faculties.

They ever wished her to do a thesis on some age old topics like, 'Hospital', 'Campus design', 'Housing' or many other things as such and also a shear fact was known: that topic was challenging their credibility and professional work style.

***

It was the rare winters on last day of the year, Trisha stayed back at my apartment to discuss the thesis' synopsis presentation. It was a one BHK studio apartment; generally, the dining space remained occupied by my drawings and literary documentations. She used to work in my bedroom. Normally, I slept on floor making few bargains for the bedding.

I went asleep sooner than normal schedule that day; there had been painstaking site visits for past three days in an interior design project. I had been unable to sleep, and stay in serenity. It was around an hour due for New Year to march in.

"I'm going to sleep dear; the site visits have killed me. Maggie is lying there in the cupboard, please help yourself if needed," I said getting down on the bedding bargain.

"Ok, but are you sure? You don't want to eat more?" She asked me, concentrating at the sketchpad. She was preparing sketches and was documenting as well.

I stared her for few fraction of a minute; she looked terrific in the long white shirt of mine and micro mini blue jeans shorts. Her curly long black hair kissed the bed while she sat, her full crimson lips were shining juicy and inviting for a deep kiss, her visible curves blanketed with sparse clothing, which were appealing for some movements and touches, and her fairness was antonymous for the last beautiful night of the year. Some bubbles started arising in my proclivity and nerves had started binding tighter.

I gulped saliva, blinked eyes for a change and said, "Nah, I'm not hungry. I ate till throat during dinner. I really need to sleep, I'm not feeling well."

"Why? What happened?" She asked with a cupid smile, she placed pencil in between her lips. She had read my eyes.

"Nothing… Goodnight!" I said lying on the bedding taking eyes off her and put quilt all over me. I was acting very different that day.

"However, I have a New Year bombshell for you," she said.

"Ok, give me the surprise tomorrow, a very Happy New Year to you in advance. Now, ponder on your work," I said in an emotionless tone and closed my eyes, soon sleep oozed me.

Temperature had fallen lot lower than the normal winters of Nagpur. It was around seven degrees as shown by my smart phone.

I was travelling deep into the fantasylands. The odd sleep of an Architect is universally accepted to be very sound and pleasing as it is the rarest of occasion when he finds one. Suddenly, I found some soft slender cold thing running through my chest and brushing protein fibers, I was also able to feel wet warm gesture on my forehead while something pulpy was crushing against my chest. I was soon to my senses, I opened my eyes. My mouth was shut by her hands, asking me not to articulate even a word.

"Happy New Year," she said hugging me tightest. I wrapped my arms around her waist. Now she was lying above me. We both looked into each other's eyes; I suddenly put down the switch besides me. It was all dark then, though moon and the celebratory crackers were spreading little light into the room that was behaving the same as how sparse white icing would have on a chocolate cake. She brought her face closer and nearer, our lips almost touched.

"I love you!" I said, and placed my thirsty orifice on her scandalous scarlet petals. We closed our eyes feeling the avid kiss. Our tongue explored deeper into our maw. We removed all differences, we were one that night.

Our lips touched everywhere; there was no barrier between us, the two lovers. Finally, I was into her, she submitted herself to me.

***

I could feel warmth on my face. Sunrays were in operation cutting off the rare affects of iciness in the 'Orange City'. I opened my eyes, I tried to rise up, but her bare arms didn't let me. We stayed there, tied among our bodies. Coverlet covered us till little above waist. I felt her smooth skin all on top of me.

"Trisha, Trisha…it is already fifteen past eight," I tried to rouse her.

"Ummm…yes. I love you Aditya," she said placing a kiss on my brow. I closed my eyes. Abruptly some wet pearls dripped on my chest, I opened my eyes.

"Hey! Dear, why are you lamenting?" I said brushing away her tears.

"I love you a lot, and I can't live devoid of you. I want to be yours perpetually throughout the life," she said hugging me.

"I love you too dear. Don't worry, we will be together even beyond the last pant. I will marry you as soon as your graduation is going to be completed," I said, caressing her ruddy cheek.

She nodded and again started kissing, she plucked my lips. We again got into a passionate lovemaking. It was already nine by then. We finally got out of the bed, I had my classes to have follow up and she had to work a lot for the thesis.

***

A beautiful fold had arrived in my life. I had found my partner. It was indeed a matter of acute bliss, and to me it seemed a landmark.

So many things had got a shuddery start in my life and the starts were demarcating, necessity and the most eventful in the graceful New Year. Trisha's family and I had already been very familiar with each other. They had started looking at me as a family man itself. It had been a regular convention for her family to invite me in all their functions and events. Trisha had already given indications to her parents. It always seemed, aunty would be the most happiest mother to dispense Trisha's hand in mine.

My architectural consultancy was on full flow as well, by then three residences and a restaurant were erected to full. The designs had befallen the way to appreciation by clients and so many big architectural critics. Many had begun claiming me to be the 'Architect of future'. The buildings were minimalistic by the use of materials and looks, all of them responded too well to the climate and the local urbanization.

But somewhere fire had to begin. That approach of design was leaving client to invest very less, yet alluring aesthetics and super sustainable micros. The Architects around had started finding it as a thorn, indeed it was cutting off so much of fees. My method was tumbling project cost by around thirty percent, so was the fees.

Many biggies had already been taunted by many clients, "Aditya sir is providing great designs at such a low price, and that too he is deeply involved, irrespective of the scale project he owns. He has been providing drawings of minute things like door hinges even."

Every cloud has a silver lining, very often the silver line proves a bit too heavy and brings Momentary collapse and hence a downfall.

`On the other hand, admiration and domino effect all around were proving my worth as a 'Teacher', post to my teaching, students had developed a passion for the subject that I taught.

Students had clearly understood, passion is the driving force behind aptitude, and, aptitude ever, is the key for practical success in the long run.

The revolution had spread brightly in the courtyard of the college where I was teaching; however, I was still worried for all other universities, institutes, schools around the Nation and globe away from my reach.

After having executed the effects to some extent there, it was well understood, lots of supremacy is needed for what I wish to achieve, and all youth need to strive ahead with this common goal.

❑

5. Meeting the sinner

It was a fresh morning; I was sitting in Chandrakant Sir's cabin browsing through various curriculums of different universities. I was really astonished to see a wide scale differences among all. It was a real fun to see drastically 'poles apart' courses of study for the same profession. Sir soon thrived in.

"Hello! What's up champ?" This is how he often to address me. He appreciated me a lot both as a teacher and as an architect.

"Nothing much sir, I was just gazing into the course of study for various universities. And, I'm flabbergasted to go through them. We have so different sets for similar course. It is real fun and a poignant fact at the same time," I said, closing the laptop's flap.

"This is an irony of the situation mate; all are sitting here only for the reason to earn, may be by any means. Might be we need to reach till the root. But, we don't know where exactly the root lies?" said Prof. Chandrakant Sir, wiping off sweat on his forehead, "Why is this damn AC not working? It's so scorching here."

"Might be, cell of remote has got discharged utterly," I said, giving a look while holding the remote in hand.

Sir buzzed the call bell to call any of the office boys. "Sir, I'm leaving for now. I have got my class of Acoustics in fourth year," I said standing off the chair.

"Ok, but meet me before departure. I'm to tell you about a competition for a new Township to be projected here in Nagpur," he said, turning over few pages of the 'Handbook of Council of Architecture'. I replied with a positive node wearing a gesture smile and left.

I met him after the class got over. He handed over the competition summary to me. It was a competition by one of the major builder group of India. They wished to build a rambling township in an area of four and a half acres of land. I was crammed with balloons of glee, I thanked sir from bottom of the heart and left.

From the moment, I was introduced by the project, I had started dreaming to win that competition by hook or crook. It was indeed a venture where I would have been able to bring up to the public, my scientific architectural propensity, a rarest of the attributes for an architect. I was dying to initiate.

***

I happily drove bike straight to Trisha's home. I wanted to tell her about the upcoming aspect at an earliest possible. I had been seeing her as my 'Lucky charm' and indeed she was happening one to be.

"Where are you? I'm standing near the shoes of your apartment building."

She replied, "I'm at my flat, come up here. See in my loggia above."

I peeped above; she was there in the balcony holding the plate of her ever favorite 'water melon'. I waved her, she waved back. She postured, calling me above.

I parked motorbike in the stilt and dashed to the lift. Thank god! Guard was absent, might be he would have gone out for the pee session. I dashed into the lift, pressing the fourth floor's button. I got out in a rush, I was over excited to tell damsel about what I was on verge to achieve. I got into her apartment. She always appears more gorgeous than the last meet. It happened then too. The queen looked amazingly beautiful in her black long top and a knee heighted grey skirt. She had her hair tied in a knot; a very pleasant sweet fragrance was making its appearance. It seemed she was just out after a bath.

I asked about her family members. She said that, they have gone out to attend a marriage observance and won't be coming before it's very late at night. Saying this she moved towards the kitchen to keep her plate. I followed, and hugged her. She kept on washing the plates in sink, as I kept on caressing her ear and hair.

I brought my lips closer to her ear, pecked there and softly said, "I love you! I have an opportunity to try my skills in a large project of township."

She turns around and says, "Wow dear, it is real amazing. I love you so much. You deserve many more such acclamations, and also you deserve lots and lots of love." She hugged me tighter accompanying a chortle.

My slender posture made some cracking sounds. She never bothered and kept pushing herself into me. Suddenly, I felt dampness on my shoulder. The shirt was wet by her precious pearls. She was slobbering as well.

"Hey, why are you crying?" I asked bringing her face in front of mine.

I ran my fingers on her cheek to peel off the precious pearls. In the process, I started quenching my thirst. She drew her face away, and said making sobering noise, "These are the tears of happiness, I'm proud of you. So lucky I'm to have you." She again dashed her head into my chest hiding her beauty.

"Dear, certainly I'm luckier one to find such an adorable supportive soul-mate like you. Even the best of the prince, and heroes would be getting resentful of me," saying this, I broke into a casual chuckle. She accompanied as well. I gave a peck on her forehead before finally getting separated. She again started washing utensils, while I searched for some eatables in the refrigerator but unfortunately Trisha had emptied it full.

"I'm in the drawing room, watching television. Come soon," I said and proceeded towards.

She joined me after few minutes, while my eyes were darted into the IBN live. It was flashing yet again, crappy, shitty change brought by HRD ministry. They were talking about a proposal, to have a common entrance test for all the engineering colleges present in India, inclusive of IITs, NITs, IIITs, BITs and various other so many. She sat beside me, resting her folded arms on my shoulder. I just spared a momentary stare and again got my eyes struck to the news relating to coverage on 'Education ruining campaign'.

"So, they are proposing a common jammed up entrance test," she shared her understanding.

I replied with a nod and said, "all these politicians are either thief or prevalent of the fools. Why don't they understand, there is no point creating dilution in pattern and adding complexity to admissions. Whatever amendments, these fools formulate, always make greater chances for the coaching institutes. Many times, I feel all these ministers, biggies of education; administrators are the cousin thieves." I spoke in a stretch and agitator pitch.

"Eat these water melons and stay cool," she said forwarding the plate to me, "and, at times, think about me too, instead of sparing our valued time listening to those, whom you call 'fools'."

I sprawled my arms, tying her in a passionate hug. I smiled and said, "Yes dear, hilarious is the situation. More we need professionals; more dilution flavor is being toned in. I'm worried." Saying this I planted a peck on red petals and soon there was not even the vacuum between us.

I dragged her to the bed, and was lying completely over her. Each masculine, met its feminine. Lovemaking lasted for next an hour, unknowing of the happenings around. Our breath was running brisk and fast, as the final assault occurred. I dashed away, lying on the bed; hand stationed on the temple, demarking the fatigue, null attire for both of us. She starts running her fingers through the hair of my chest, while a snowy quilt overcastted our organization. January waft was brushing our top, but, the heat of our love was able to outcast it.

"Oops! It's too late, Mom, Dad and others would be coming back soon," she said looking at the wall clock, which hummed hourly chrome, and merely an hour remained for the midnight to fall in. We got up in a hurry, and put on our dressings properly. I left kissing her goodbye.

***

I could not sleep properly that night, thoughts of past were clanging me deep. I remembered it well, how the transformations of system had eaten up my aspirations, dreams, and desires. I always wished to be an IITan, might be that time, it was an urge as I wanted to prove my worth of self-studies.

Ultimately, the claimers had won and I was defeated.

There saga to yell: One can never make it to IIT without being coached was proven. Never they thought ever, what the reason was? I wished they ever appreciated me cracking the screening, but, then too it was like a war to them: War of ideology and principles.

Alas! Had they not made IIT a onetime affair, relying on

the age-old pattern of screening then the mains, I might have been an IITan. This comes a little on selfish part, but the truth remains: *that twist ate up whatever bright premiere school did hold, since then the quality has been falling.*

This did nothing good to IIT but opened enormous scope for farting coaching institutes. They did add- a student can make only a couple of attempts, that too in a continuous stretch from his class twelve and a student needs minimum 60% of marks to be eligible to appear. It was the real fun of the system. Why does one need to bother about student's marks in class twelve, if he is able to crack the so conceptual, harsh and terrific problems in JEE entrance?

That had an evil message- *coaching is the key, in scarcity of time.*

Then onwards, students had to work hardest for class twelve boards as well as the entrance exams as mutually they relied on different course pattern and content. How beautiful the issue would have been if students had to study subjects, rather than preparing for parametric tests coming up head. I wonder for educationalist's making and upbringing, what did they eat that they have such a mean and squat solicitous brain?

I was already very low and numb thinking for the slurry part of past. I was also feeling very bad imagining of the hopeless hands driving the Nation's bus. I could never know when before dashing in land of dreams and fantasies.

***

Time, time, time, time...oh my god, it never waits. The cut-off date for submission was looming. I was concentrating deep on the township project. I was all set to dry in wool to be commissioned for that venture. It never seemed an easy task for a single man army, being the sole Architect of the firm. Though few students were seeking some exertion opportunities with me as my lectures had always proven matter of delight to them and they wanted to see the happenings practically as well.

Trisha was unable to facilitate me this time because of the coming date for her thesis submission. Finally, after working wholeheartedly a decade of days, Proposal Presentation came organized. Lot many proposals by the biggies of architecture was sought to be tabled, weak nerve was to temp in for sure.

"Here it is sir!" I said after showing presentation to Chandrakant sir for his approval.

"Very well done Aditya, but another face of metal currency can't be ignored...well, I guess it may fall a little on hypothetical cliff upfront to those who are to conclude," sir said pointing fingers at the monitor. His eyes squeezed among self, hinting the taunting doubt pacing up. Impartial fear followed momentary happiness, but confidence to cross by hurdles was high as well.

"It is well understood by me, sir. They may find project unfeasible considering the past they could touch," I further tried to convince him, "being the pioneer creator, I hold the key too. Indeed the chit code lies with me. I can make it happen. I will describe the viability formulae and its special feature to reduce project cost in view of long run once the interrogation is modeled. Not only this, after my idea behind, its construction gets explained, many giants of field may then realize-they committed crime by erasing the importance of basic science from ever adorable 'Architecture-Curriculum.'"

"Hmm...ok go ahead," sir wished me luck pushing his thumb up. This time his smirk had lots of eulogize and encouragement. I responded with a petite smile.

***

Next day was a big one; sleep was miles away that night. I remained stuck to bed, watching the chocolaty trio blades churning warm air back to me. The fact projected by Prof. Chandrakant was taunting me then.

How can we Architects be so unrealistic, airy and illiterate at mathematical sciences, it is known: *Architecture is a mother of all art, but all art indeed are offspring of Mathematics and Architecture together.*

The blades churning above had been yelling this from long, if Architects would have known science then they never ever would have proposed it on top. Breaking the thought underlying silence, phone buzzed. It was my love there.

"Why didn't you call me whole day, I had been waiting long," she complained, "don't you have time for me even," she sobered sarcastically.

"No dear, nothing as such. I was busy, with the presentation whole day. I'm presenting it tomorrow, I'm worried for the outcome," I said, holding the breath.

"Oh yes. I'm sorry, I could not even contribute a little to your work. But, it must be superbly *Adian* design. Moreover, I'm so sure about it," she said childishly in a blissful tenor.

"For this some prize must be presented then," I said spreading a cunning smile, "might be you can pour in sweetest nectar, the priceless gift."

"Hmm...yeah, you will get your gift soonest darling," we talked late that night, though upcoming cock-crow was an important one. I had to be all to my senses for the falling day.

***

An intelligent known crowd of around two century was present in the lecture hall. Nine of the ten Architects had already been through there presentations. The chatty feedback had been proving the efficiency and effectiveness of their works. Many had concluded for the project lying at the hands of either Ar.Munshir or Ar.Derendra, both of them were well known for big townships and real estate projects, though I never found their works serving the credibility of Architects. I had heard, both being among the biggest manipulators of building by-laws and regulations even. What a mockery? Yet they were "The One" to be praised ones!

After discussion and presentation session of quad hours, my turn came. The last of all, I could see least interest among the audience and critic. Might be; my age and last status kept them uninterested. I presented the proposal, which seemed twister and unrealistic to most of them.

"Why do you want to accommodate the small vendors from *Buildi Market* as a part of commercial zone of this township? These seem so weird and nonsense real estate approaches," fingered one of the critics, "Why don't you let *Buildi* remain how it is? Instead of worrying for the city problems: *what you call*. Better solve ours; the builder's concern." The hall had again turned little lively, with the sudden murmur. Few of them had started shining their teeth with giggling sign of dishonor.

"That is so true sir! I'm here to serve you with best of the designs proposals and I did the unchanged. After you bring in those vendors as a part of this township, the social life will be maintained and at the same time this will make you earn lot more business turnover. We can also help our city by overcoming the underlying problem of congestion through a patch using this scheme. Investment falls little higher initially but very worthy considering long run." I said, trying to explain critics and owners the underlying metabolism.

"You are very hypothetical and airy with your design. Son, we are here to invest what Architects don't earn even for whole of their career. Grow up!" cried one of the other partner builders.

"Sir, we are adding lots of credibility by doing it. The city's major planning fault will be eradicated by applying these calculations. Moreover, the kind of trendy shopping arcades and complex you are seeking to build will be dry life out. All of us, irrespective of class, prefer street shopping; none wish to pay an extra on any commodity. The shopping malls sell many articles at higher domain of prices and again there are lots of complexities. We have already witnessed the failure of Empress City Mall; we must not bring another junk as such. We often forget Urban Heat Island while dealing project architecturally. It is very simple, why to build if things can be solved staying beneath four trees," I tried explaining the need, "We often disregard, whatever we build is ultimately affecting ecosystem as a whole. Mother earth is weeping, but the thick spectacle has made the tear remain invisible. This is the time to react or else all will be ruined."

"Enough of speech, beliefs and concept don't ascertain execution. Your design too seems very much non-executive. Please explain a little about its erection methodology, and then let's see, if at all something works out," said the chief of builder.

"Yeah, sure! Well the township is to be designed in a very singular manner; I never witnessed such situations before in my whole career until now. We will be applying the scheme of cut and fill to generate the manifesto. The excavated earth material is to be used for building artificial landmass, below which the indigenous vendors will be placed. The overlapping earthwork is to take hold of the modern township and commercial built masses. What this does is that maintains the difference in geographical location of two distinct bargains but psychologically gives the feeling of unity among all," I said passing by through the slides.

The explaNation proved yet again a stunner beamer, and indeed, they could not take it at all.

It's a sad fact, when something falls nail bitter for acclaimed laureates they have nothing else to say but, "Again, you are getting a bit too prosaic. We have to build this proposal this birth itself. We don't have all seven births in hand to execute, be practical kid. My experience says- what you are proposing is merely wastage of our precious time and airy in nature."

Questions kept coming to me; I kept trying my best to explain the design. Unfortunately, my design was falling on the principles of high profiled scientific application, which was clearly not understood by so many able architectural heads and builders sitting there.

Ultimately, I was lost at the hands of sinners.

The world seems so hypocrite, you teach big theories and big talks during academics which you yourself fear to apply in real life. And then you exclaim- Academic life is vastly different from the practical one.

Then my question is- *What for a student pays in the form of fees throughout the academic career if teaching during that phase is practically in-applicable?*

❑

6. The holy bath

The failure indeed is a tangy awakener and at many occasions, it comes out to be a best preacher. Same concourse of verbs happened with me, I had already realized the urge of reformation in noble profession through wee hours bash.

I was walking by the footpath, which ran through the locality of Laxmi-Nagar; it was sparsely some moments due for another patch of day to fall by. Birds were paddling back to nests, while office goers were clearly seen with the puff of happiness and pleasure for being home which was easily visible on each face; their haste was adding icing to the bakery of evening.

I too was returning back home, but as a contrast my feet were walking slower than deliveries of a spinner, if other's movement was as paced as bowling by *Rawalpindi Express*. I wished to get dug within the manholes around; the cry of pain had so low frequency that I was not even able to notice vibrations and melody in my pocket. Elongated continuation brought me back into the world, Trisha was calling. I pressed my lower lip overlapping the upper one, intent hinted not to respond. But somewhere heart was searching for a shoulder to cry upon.

This was not, what she had in appetite of anticipation, I broke into flashing pain indicator, carefree about the populace around, and I was howling aloud.

"Hey dear, please don't cry? You are a brave man…these are small issues. A man of your caliber weeping worst than a lass doesn't justify," it was understood to her. I never cared to share this painful happening with my parents even, there I was walking as a loser as thought, searching for some space to hide worthlessness.

"It's all gone Trisha. It seems to be all faked, why did I

learn the way I did? Why they called me the 'Change Creator', 'The Rebel Architect'?" I kept crying on the phone, all the trace passers were getting full trace of me.

"Good things come with time Adi, who can know this better than you? Come on, chill up now and come down to my place. We will go out for a coffee break at your favorite café," Trisha tried making me smile within one of the patches achieved in my life.

I slowed pace of my howl, but kept sobering and said, "I don't feel like going anywhere dear. It seems whole world is laughing aloud at me. I still have no clues to face Prof. Chandrakant."

"It's very fine. You are bit too exaggerating and presuming the issues, Prof. Chandrakant knows you well, isn't? Why will he question for this loss. You have won by losing. It's better not to do the projects for such crooked people. What if you would have been assigned to do the project and then they would have shown their real color during the ongoing of project. Then problems would have been serious and worst even."

"Hmm…might be. Alright, we will talk more about it when we seat together," I said wiping handkerchief through my nose and eyes.

We both spent some great moments together at café near Law College Square. Trisha tried making me understand so many aspects of life, with different angles.

World always seemed so much pure and clear to me before, but in reality, practical world involves complexities added by sinners.

What we are taught in childhood is never applied by elders themselves because it only means chapters of books to them, which help fetch marks to their kid.

I came home late that night. Trisha's words had brought lots of refreshment to me. Yet, I was very disturbed because of the variety of populace I met, the *Sinners*.

I took an hour-long shower, remained unmoved with closed eyes. The moments were flashing back to my brain through the time. I badly wanted to flush them off, but it was falling very sturdy to get away with it.

I got into my bedroom after the bath, just with the tied towel at the name of cloth. Dejections and only disappointments seemed present all around in the form of all degree, credentials, medals and pictures hanging on the wall. The Aditya of today, wanted to shred off all of them in a while.

I wish, I never had met those people, and then at least halluciNation would have kept me happy for long.

I couldn't hold on with the rage, I brought down all pictures from the wall and banged it hard on the floor. The glass frame scattered into pieces, my brain was looking for more disaster. I stepped ahead, it pained like a cut, but I never cared. I reached to the degree hanging on wall, but soon phone started buzzing. I took away my hand from the hanging degree; it was only an inch away from getting ravished.

I unwantedly picked the phone falling in compulsion. Prof. Chandrakant was on line.

"What happened to the presentation? I'm sorry as I missed it," said Professor.

"It's alright sir, no issues that you couldn't be there," I took a halt and said, "You were correct sir. I failed in front of them."

"Oh...no issues Aditya, it's fine that you got exposed to realistic field of real estate, and there will be numerous opportunities coming ahead, along with the same shade of populace, next time be prepared." The professor tried consoling me.

We talked for some times, he kept boosting me, but I was in some other trance, all the way thinking about my design, their perspective and the un-ethical practical world.

With the time, this pain started healing, but it had formed a big dark mark, which was never to be removed. However, the mark or scare indeed helps generating recognition. I'm still waiting for that identification.

I had started practicing Architecture in a full flow. Now there were no big real estate projects but all small residences and bungalows. Practicing this way also, I came to discern so many brutal realities. Clients have a very vague perspective of what an architect does. I came across many clients, who stopped responding to my calls and emails, post to getting initial layouts, presentation drawings and submission drawings. I did seven big projects in a small span of four months, but got paid for only one of them.

Clients often used to come up with a say that, they don't wish to build right now, so they won't be paying any fees. Then the picture was becoming clearer to me, I was getting the reasons for so many non-architecture buildings existing all around. It's very obvious any Architect won't ever work his heart out if clients will keep cheating them on a habitual note. Indeed clap does need duo of hands.

Public must respect a profession if they want a good result. No one can ever provide you the best results if you don't respect his caliber and credibility.

With so many adverse different thoughts coming from various angles, ultimately it all started forming a web. The answer was not becoming clear for whom to be blamed? Or, it was like, correcting myself will correct whole many.

❑

7. Assault initiates

Days had again throbbed in at natural pace and complexity had been far away. Lecturer kept being busy delivering lecture; Architect kept practicing his own style while the emotions were dogged to be transformed into relation. Trisha's mother felt the knots to be tied. Trisha had never told it to me, but aunty had already put the message to my birth giver.

"Yes Mummy, I'm all very good and even the work is running on a placid path," I was on a phonic conversation and the most awaited shock was to be delivered, "Adi, why you never ever cared to tell this to me?"

"What, I didn't tell to you. I can't remember any such incidence. Will you please tell me what it is?" I said wearing expressions of perplexity wrapped with the attire of aghast as well. Petite worry was reinforced too; my mood kept whispering the occurrence of losing the project and kind of humiliation I faced.

"Yes, I would have been the happiest person to know the relation between you and Trisha," sweat was all stuck to my forehead, once Mummy started explaining everything, "I was in deep shudder when Mrs. Pandey told everything to me, and not only this we have also planned to make you both engaged soon."

I kept numb and silent for a while, whereas Mummy kept checking my presence on phone, I didn't know the way to react. Two were the reason, I was indeed getting engaged as a debutant and also there was a deep dilemma between being happy and defaulter. Soon I spoke, "Eh…I'm very sorry Mummy, I was just about to explain and get permission from you but work never let me free enough," I tried responding being Mom's boy.

Always some white lotion is needed to cut the error occurred.

Finally, we concluded the talk, 23rd day of April was taken into consideration for engagement to occur. We had also been in discussion about the expected confrontation by the rest of the family members regarding issue of my marriage with Trisha. However, I was sure for one thing; if Dad gets swayed then rest won't be much of the problem. The clouds of utter happiness were showering in full flow; my brain was tricking way to keep my lord all very pleased and agreed. The time had been passing by.

All had been settled accept few jitters by the end of my family members as thought earlier. I had also informed Dad about my aspiration to be an IAS officer, who had further worked as a catalyst to get his acceptance, and the preparation had initiated as well.

I will better not like to tell much about the drama happened. Let's get forward.

***

It was the night before our engagement.

"You know Adi, I can't believe, it is happening in reality. We will be soon one…but somewhere lots of nerve stiffer is coming in as well," said Trisha while talking with me on phone.

The alligators had already made their mark by then, the zero state between night and day had just clanged in, and emotions were pretty childish juvenile. I swallowed the surfaced saliva of the throat; as never had it happened before.

"Even, I am able to feel being landed on the planet of fantasy, the day we had dreamt off long ago is coming tomorrow," I said.

***

Next day, we both were engaged in a grand function at Tuli InterNational, Nagpur. The evening was fabulous; it was over flooded with the well-wishers. All had come as part, but my eyes kept knowingly waiting for those from my blood. I knew, they won't ever come and they didn't; only Mom and Dad were present; I was hypothetically waiting for many others. Trisha's parents asked as well for the reason behind absence of rest of my family members, but I didn't had any answer other than concluding very smartly.

The great Moment was over in such a rush.

It's a truth the moments you wait longing for, don't last till long.

***

Some other big effects were to come by very soon. The real assault of my life was yet to begin. I had finally decided to take up an IAS entrance examination with the intent to provide recovery to the saline-based system of ours.

On the other end, academic system was taunting deep as well. It was only few days back when, changes in the syllabus of B.Arch of Nagpur University had come by. Experts said that it was being done only with the cause to minimize the anxiety on the brain of young kids, at times the students are in extreme pressure of academics and they are ending up with so much mental problems as well. The moment was subordinated with lots of inner giggle hearing to this. It was well known to me, the Educationalists are merely doing it with the motive to make curriculum more compatible for more and more crowd, and that day won't be far, when anyone would be going for some other profession by choice of the time. That time, they had removed Mathematics as a subject from the first year curriculum, and further more idea was to make subject of structure more concept based than calculative. I was both in state of fun and worry facing this hilarious loss.

As an alternative of focusing on increasing the excellence, India is beckoning to be a Nation with more quantity of professionals. Might be, it is the reason why; despite having maximum counts of engineer, ours is the Nation where engineers feel trepidation even to merely build a bridge more than the length of a score kilometers. No doubt, our engineers are most paid, but where are they being paid from? - The Banks, Financial Sectors and Social Networking Sites, as we have been serving multinational companies for the neglected works by foreign engineers.

Government and panel actually dilute the syllabus only so as to increase the intake, they are least bothered about the infrastructure building and development; rather they are more into their Swiss development.

After joining as a Professor, the scene was becoming much clear to me. Private colleges in Nagpur University were meanly busy, making enough of money through the quota of donation and capacitating fees, and the sad verity lies that, not even the university was interested to find the reasonable number of seats through the legal method of counseling. I came across a college that shared only 30 out of 400 seats for normal admittance process, rest were filled through the policy of management in the form of donations, and never even UGC or other affiliating and accreditation body tried to probe in.

The question, which always kept banging through my nerves was- why guardian wishes to make their kid an engineer or doctor if the vital stats say them to be non-eligible. In the dream of safeguarding their future why do they find National infrastructure and concerns as the only beads to play with?

There were lots of activities going on and I was all set to do something for it. Any bug cannot let you live long without actually finding some repellant for it.

***

Prof. Chadrakant and I were seated together discussing about the problems of the system prevailing at University.

"It is really a baseless idea to drag out subject like Mathematics from the first year of 'Architecture Education'. It will bring nothing more but Painters and Artists at the name of Architects, who will be only presenting the image of buildings without actually showing executive part of it," I shared my concern while conversing with Prof. Chandrakant.

"Yes, somewhere this is the fact my buddy. However, in this materialistic world, there is no place for the excellence. The world is full of hypocrites, who are least worried for future living, they are more into gaining momentary happiness and indeed the Nation is suffering a lot for that," Professor shared.

The channel of happenings all around was tied within as a web and each link was pointing to other. Ministry to Institutes, Institutes to Coaching Centers, Coaching Centers to Private Colleges and many as such, the cheapest businessmen were on the role.

My opinion towards days to come by was known to me. I told Chandrakant sir about my new venture. He was very happy and overwhelmed to know that. "Sir, I'm frustrated out of this system as a whole. Teachers don't let me experiment, Architects are not letting true Architecture prevail by portraying the false image of Architecture to the public, students yet want spoon feeding, students seek notes for examination, all plunge upon for grades and marks while I check there designs."

"Can you please elaborate the concern, being a little more precise?" Sir asked.

"Yes sir, sure. Frank L Wright, the legend Architect had once told, 'Architecture is truthful', but today most of the Architecture is fancied with the high end use of claddings and coverings. Stone cladding take up stone masonry and more to follow up...Not only these teachers waste most of their time calculating attendance records, teaching methodology reports but never they care how much actually students are learning practically. When it comes to the thought of practicality, students are bounded to design rectangular boxes without reinforcing the zeal of creativity. When I teach them the perfections of subject like Acoustics, they ask the ways to write in the University examinations. Students ask for grades on sheets prior to know the mistakes and goods of design they made. Gaining at a material scale has overcastted the age old concept of learning and this is precarious."

I said without any pause, as if these utters were deeply pushed within me, "Sir, not only this, I have also witnessed the projects being taken up by the Women's College of Architecture, Nagpur. They are always very hypothetical in nature, bringing no practicality good to the students. There had been an incidence last year; the fourth year batch was given to design a Philosophical Center in the time when they should have been playing with advanced services of buildings. We need to put a stop to it, or else someday the whole thing will be ruined, and only an administrator can stop it. Getting to be an educational administrator is a long deal hence farther the thought reformation, so I thought of being the one like an IAS officer."

"But mate, how will you clear the gangue particles from the compound called, 'Education System' becoming an IAS officer?" This question was put by Chandrakant sir on a concerning serious note. I was unable to present a substantial answer to him. We continued talking for sometime but soon I decided to take a leave.

"Almost immediately, the things will be clear sir…It's been too late sir, I'm leaving now, a client is waiting for me," I said and took a leave.

The interrogation by sir was very obvious and a needful one. Moreover, I didn't have the clear answer with me. The way seemed as I thought but the passing by nodes and the travel node seemed very anonymous.

***

Preparation for IAS examination had begun on full swing. The determiNation was high; the never known answers were yet to be found.

The fourth dimension of Einstein always proves brisk than all other.

The marriage time of Trisha and me was approaching. Only a month was left for the pleasure moment. Our emotional adhesiveness was soon to earn a noun projectable enough in the over powered lens of society.

We got married during the chilly winters of December. The ceremony brought adverse reasons to express for many, we two had become notch matter of discussion among the two geographically different family.

***

It was our first night after marriage almost after a year, when we had first time made love with each other. The December waft was partially making its way through the slits by the side of window frame resulting from the contraction. Incandescent lamp was pouring marvelous auspicious hued lumens while the Jasmine and Rosy fragrance was bringing the sweet highness. Trisha was sitting amid the bed surmounted by a Jasmine hung pyramidal form, while the scarlet Rose petals never allowed view of the quilt below.

She was clad in red *Lehenga*, with *Ghunghat* falling all over her portrait. I slowly put the latch to the door and stepped ahead many better than a cat, but deliberate silence didn't let it happen. The tender emotion to see my bride had turned my nerves all very fast and brisk. I stepped ahead finally stationing myself in front of her, she remained very numb. I dared not to break the serenity of silence.

I took my face closer and slowly started putting her *Ghunghat* away; she took a deep breath, which I could hear from her sizzle. Oh…beauty of all the universe seemed having thrived in her. The scarlet dot on her forehead was making her glow much more. I kept staring at her, but she never cared to interlace her eyes with mine, only happening I could witness was forcing of dribble through her throat because of the diamond necklace movement.

Irrespective of time having spent, whatever the magnitude may be the first commotion and meet after being tied in the socially accepted knot is always pleasure giving.

I raised her face, holding chin from one of the hands, and cupped her face between my palms. She looked into my eyes this time with fervent adore, I planted one, two, three…pecks on her forehead, she closed her eyes. All of a sudden, she clutched me in a hug and we remained speechless in each other's arm for long moment. 'I love you' was the only rare words being spoken in middle. Neither of us wanted to be separated.

Night was falling fast and brisk along with the thermometer. We were placed beneath the white quilt; our wedding attire remained crumpled near one of the vertices of massive beautiful bed.

We talked the whole night; indeed it was the best night of our life as even sleep too never dared to come as a hurdle between two of us. We wished that night to be infinite and to last till our last breath but reality had to win.

The glorious time was followed with another auspicious vacation, whose reminiscence, I never wished to be erased from my memoir of nerves.

Trisha and I went to Trivandrum for our honeymoon, the moments spent there, became metal carved reminiscences. There, we took up a resolution to spend similar time at many other serine places of India every year during the same dates to keep memories alive and fresh, but it…just couldn't happen again.

We had shifted to a newly purchased apartment in the locality known as Manish Nagar, where our new life took its birth.

❑

8. IAS brings Kartik

We both had been thoroughly engaged in settling the things to the proper state, owing to an urgent shifting. Trisha was very happy to get a new apartment as a gift from me; it was indeed a new commencement for both of us. We had started using it as a composite house; my life partner was now also my business collaborator.

The life had achieved a level of beauty and the synonym of a common man's settlement, but Aditya's soul had some other demands. My routine had changed a lot in the time to come by, the whole day was devoted to the Architecture and teaching while most of the night time was for an elite dream.

***

On the other edge, some other improvements were stirring in full pour. Few students at the college had placed a petition against me for not giving an examination-oriented-teaching. The spoon feeding trend with an urge to heave marks on shitty statement papers, had badly spoiled the future of today, and they were the same students, those once used to enjoy my preaching.

"Aditya, what is happening? This is for the first time when students are complaining for not getting the adequate study materials and they are really worried for their examinations," concern and worry seemed stacked within the conversation of the Principal.

"This is not the actual fact, sir. I have tried my best to make their concept crystal clear and apparent. If the concepts are done with a little eagerness to perform then any related problem can be easily sorted out. Moreover, not only the questions of examination, even the practical hurdles find its eased removal once a student relies on knowing the realm of the topic taught," I tried, clearly explaining to Mr. Principal.

It was a real fact, I ever tried making students realize worth of knowledge over marks and degree but unfortunately both oldies as well as contemporaries were unable to find innovation as key to success. Must have been two reasons for the oldies, college runs on strength of students along with university merit list or might have they not been able to realize or comprehend my doings.

"That is well understood to me Aditya, but still, try to supervise the things on their part. Examinations are as important as practical knowledge and understandings," he giggled, and patted his hands on my shoulder, "I have lots of experience and most of the times, it is correct."

This time you are wrong, or might be you intentionally are getting wrong…thoughts are one of those chattels, which don't fear or get paused for any uphill ahead.

"Alright, sir! But, I want to inform something to you…I'm appearing in Civil Services examinations for IAS Cadre this year… I need lots of blessings from you," I conveyed.

"Oh, wow! This is a pleasure for all of us, "Principal said wearing a smile, I never knew and felt if it was witty, cupid or praise giver. However, I took it as the third opinion, and left from the cabin saluting goodbye greetings.

I doubted if he would have read my intention, I was just sharing the possibility of leaving the college teachings.

***

The globe, kept performing gyratory and revolution through the usual pace, and many twists kept being planned through the phase.

"Darling, I have cleared the written examination and the personal interview is scheduled after a couple of months," I numbly spoke, tapping through the pad of laptop. She was lying beside me on the bed, our backs were tucked perpendicularly to the bottom body half. Her head was placed on my shoulder, while eyes tried finding some sleep.

"Hmm..." she replied, her eyes were being shut by then. The aroma of sleep was all high on her. I kept numb for some time and then, helped her to a proper sleeping posture. The night had almost reached the state of darkest, and in some while bliss of day was to ascend.

***

"Adi...Adi, you are already very late...wake up, only few minutes are remain due for your lecture."

"Umm..." I removed the quilt over my body, stretched my hands against gravity and pulled the eye shutter partially. The honey-lured hangover was still on, and even some naughty lover lived within me. I caught hold of Trisha's hand just the moment, she turned taking leave from nearby...she stopped, and there I pulled her towards me. Now, she was there in my arms.

The climate seemed very pleasant and winy. The cozy smell of earth was reaching my nostrils, as the almighty's shower was falling with full grace. Moreover, the trapping fumes from my damsel, was outdoing me to carry on with jobs ahead.

A white *saree* was wrapped all around her, and the red dot on her forehead was so beautifully complementing the brightest whitish with long curly hairs almost ending at the height of windowsill.

She smiled and turned around, we faced each other. Our optical rays kept fluttering between our eyes. It was all silent around if the music of pouring rain is dejected, though I was able to perceive the melody of heartbeats. Nevertheless, I never counted; the feelings articulated it, getting beyond *seventy-two* per minutes. The aroma of her hair and body made me close my eyes and sense the eternity through the soul. Unseeingly, I could sense the heat around my lips, and soon warm sweet taste made a way through it. We were now in a deep embrace and she never felt like pinning me any more for the lecture to come by. All among us was synchronized with a mammoth catalyst from the reaction of adore. The movement of muscles and the negligent air gap between us *the duo* had become the reason for us turning into trio.

The time, we became two from solitary, breath was heavy at motion while a sign of completeness remained on her face. She puffed my two days bearded cheek and smiled.

All of a sudden, mobile buzzed. Screen flashed, a call was coming from the Head of the Department. I made a talk with him, and soon realized of getting very late. Only scores of minutes remained for the lecture to begin.

"Oh, I need to go dear...it's alarmingly very late. I was also sacked last week for getting late to the lecture of Working

Drawing," saying this, I jumped from the bed and pounced lined to the washroom.

"I had been waking you up since an hour, but you…" she broke into a giggle. I followed her with one, and got in to get ready. I was rapidly geared up and having the breakfast together.

"You know, only PI and GD remains between me and IAS officer," I said, padding butter on bread.

"Wow! That is so amazing…but how do care to inform me so late? The news must have come yesterday only," she replied wearing frown on her beautiful portrait.

I frowned back and replied, "I had manners to inform you last night itself, but someone had to sleep at best."

She smiled and put her head down with a sense of shame and said, "Oh really…I'm so sorry dear," she forwarded her lips and planted a kiss on my cheek.

I took hold of her wrist, and said, "It is all because of you dear, my lucky charm. Had you not been in my life, success won't have come running to me."

She smiled in a blush and said, "You remember, I had once told, 'good things come with time'. By the way, you too have worked your heart out for this, which is the ultimate reason behind this."

I soon finished the breakfast, talked in a brisk and rushed to the college for my lecture. A minimum of half an hour delay was for sure.

***

Tick…tick…tick…clock hands never befall, nor sun ever got late and life kept running with normal pace with few abnormalities and happiness ahead. Trisha had been examined to be pregnant, and she was to deliver my piece of heart in some days around. Trisha was shifted to her own house, to avoid any complications. In the meanwhile, I had taken over the 'Personal Interview' and 'Group Discussion' session of IAS examination. They went very slickly, though I had stopped thinking for the results, deeds had become prime focus for me.

***

I was struck in the college as usual.

"Congratulations Aditya! You have once again made us proud on you," Head of the department said shaking hands with me. He had made one of the rarest appearances in my cabin and I was overwhelmed to receive him.

"Please have a seat sir," I smiled back and said, "What happened sir?" things seemed mysterious to me.

"Huh…you don't know yet. You have topped in the finals of the IAS examination," he said draining a smile followed with a usual frown.

"Really…" my mouth turned wide open sequenced with a deep smile, "Thanks a ton sir and I'm very sorry…"

"Hey hey…its very fine Aditya, now don't be seated, go and fetch some sweets," he said patting me on my back.

"Yes sir…sure," I said and left out of the place. In a shudder my phone buzzed, it was a phone call by Trisha's Mom. I picked the call delightfully with the intent to share the good news with her, but some very different juvenile emotions came in after having a talk with her. Trisha had been admitted owing to the labor pain. It was a matter of extreme delight for me, after long big reason to smile huge had come. I remained speechless to hear but soon replied with lots of delightful words. I was extremely nervous out of enthusiasm and happiness. I started laughing and giggling in self, my activities were matching to the brilliance of a tranquilizer consumer and rushed whole-heartedly to the hospital. Although despite the extreme happiness to get the junior, my brain was also stuck in the fear for complications cloud overlaying Trisha.

When I reached to the hospital, all from Trisha's home and few friends of her were present at the opening of operation theatre. All faces looked dual expressional.

Life had been giving me awkwardness with the puffs of glee since long, here I was selected as an IAS, a dream came true but on the other edge, Trisha was struggling to bring the new one. Overcasting both was the happiness of standing on verge of becoming Father… Happiness, worries, glee…anonymous emotions existed all around.

"I tried calling you numerous epochs Adi, but all the times your phone seemed away from coverage area," Trisha's Mom came screaming at me, sense of worry reflected clearly in her words.

"I'm very sorry Mummy; I'm stationed at a very far off

outskirts, where phone network hardly connected. Anyway, how is Trisha? When was she admitted?"

We exchanged our words for sometimes, but soon surgeon appeared in the prospect.

***

"Congratulations to all of you. Trisha has just delivered a boy, and both of them are in good health," doctor said coming out of the operation theatre, "Can I please see Mr. Sinha? Some formalities need to be finished." A smile followed.

All faces broke into a sudden smile and started thanking almighty. I pounced to the doctor very happily and ardently, and asked, "Sir, how is Trisha now? Can I meet her and the baby now, Doctor?"

"Oh! Mr. Sinha. Congratulations! Yes you can definitely meet both of them, but prior to that please come with me for some paperwork…hardly for few minutes. Moreover, if I have not gone wrong Mr. Sinha, you are the same person who has topped the IAS examination," doctor said and shook hands with me wearing a pleasing smile, "I had seen the result in the newspaper of today's morning."

"Thanks a lot sir," I said and started walking along with him for the formalities; I was in a rush to remove all cliff hanger to meet Trisha and my son at an earliest. The emotion for the moment were very naïve, unexplainable…for long, I had been provided the best as a son, and now time had come to give the best to my own son.

***

All disgraces of the past had got blemished in the moments, which had begun with Kartik, my son. However, I had to get alienated from both Trisha and Kartik, as my six months IAS training program was due to begin within some days.

Trisha never wished to let me go so early but even she knew what that severance meant to all. I never knew when the two months flew away, and I had to leave.

After scrupulous training period at the allotted *crade*, I was recruited to Hazaribagh, my hometown as the first posting. New venture always brings excitement and nervousness to begin with, but when determiNation is high, green consequence seems to be very near.

❑

9. Home tastes bitter

The new venture had just begun. It is always a matter of delight for every father when his kid fulfils the dream his grandfather had once seen for his son. My grandfather always wished my Dad to become an IAS officer.

Though so called 'fortune' often cheats the strong, but the well said phrase is- 'fortune favors the brave'.

My Dad had prepared his heart out and *dyed in wool*, but almighty was conspiring for some other happenings. Unfortunately, the papers of examination had burnt to ashes and the examination was abandoned. Good thing was that, it lead my father to become a teacher, which gave me many reasons to see the day, I saw later.

***

The enchanting mechanical sound of the iron wheels, and conveyer belt was this time not walking by my journey. The melody was unheard as the atmosphere-controlling compartment doesn't let in any nature reality. Beautiful, dark and dense hair of Mother Nature was spread all around. Still, I was unable to perceive and feel the devine beauty; the fluttering image of artificial inside had deeply overlaid the damsel.

When you travel alone, there are so many colorful thoughts of past and future projections, which overwhelm one's brain for sure. The same was happening with me, I was unable to drag my focus towards partially visible beauty outside, which must have mesmerized any of my type.

Still, I never see it to be the failure of 'nature', as it remains the way it is, glass is though transparent as called, but the objects all around out-do its basic character which is to, let light in.

I stayed, gluing my face to the glass pane; the transparent barrier though never let me touch the serine beyond. How dull and dumb I was, during my school days, never would have ever thought the story that was to be scripted soon. Hilarious and inspiring that moment seems, when my relatives had been declaring an urgent need for me to join coaching or tuition institutes in order to avoid the consequence, which never occurred, though I never heard their say. I scored 100% in Mathematics and further carried on as a researcher in the same field. However, happy fact for me was that, I was campaigning against what they wished me to do and they appeared wrong to me every way, despite their intention was as clean as a vodka peg. The realm of non-needed wrong tradition thought, never stopped there, interrogations also fell in when my grades fell low, though I was learning designs well.

I don't know why the so called 'Elders' never understood or ever tried understanding that, the major bunch of marks generators are only those, who were able to mug up the whole questions bank well before few days to examination and then do those muggers really remember all when needed to apply in the field? Sad fact is, they again need books to refer, because they never learnt the subject, process of learning was deep buried by the overweight of 'Short-cut to degree', and we are still paying off today.

While my thought kept getting plunged in the pool of yesterdays and related future improvisations, sleep was there, captivating in as well. I rolled down on the side lower berth, and put off the lamp above.

"Who is there? Put the lamp on," a young teen masculine voice appeared from top, "Can't you see I'm studying for my examination," enough arrogance was there in the voice, which just poured in.

I put back the lamp on, wearing a gentle smile, came hanging out of my berth and holding the upper berth in an orangutan style, I saw, there was a young lad who appeared to be a teenager. His eyes were stuck to sample papers, given by any coaching institute while earphone was pushed into his ear. His feet were tapping, perhaps in synchronization with the beats through music player. He wore a pant, longer than, to be called shorts and shorter to be called a full pant, which was yellow chrome in shade and the shirt was white in color, which had an image of some foreign rock-star.

I politely and smilingly asked, "What are you studying and what for?" smile was there on a contrast to the annoying frown, which came up from his end.

"I'm preparing for IIT-JEE entrance examination. It is a very alleged examination almost parallel to IAS," he emphasized.

"Oh really! I never knew so," I replied with pickled sense, "It is great that you are preparing for one of the greatest examinations. However, as far as my limited knowledge is concerned, we need the knowledge of subjects to clear any examination and that indeed should be the motto. I can't see any subjective book in your hand."

"As I told you, it is not that easy, we need to prepare through sample question papers and get aid from coaching institutes, which coaches us well for the examination," he said wearing a overconfident smile, "and the book, which you see in my hand is a set of sample papers given by one of the leading coaching institutes."

I concluded the talk with a smile and a goodnight greeting. Indeed arguing with him would have not lead to any positive result apart from shear loss of yelling energy at both ends. I was soon trapped into the arms of dream giver lady and thoughts, philosophies and wishes had by then taken form of fantasies.

Suddenly, my eyes opened, facing a sudden jerk. I peeped through the glass pane. The train was holding at the destined station. I was amazed for the sound sleep, which had thronged me. I waited for the whole train to get emptied; I got down, holding my two large bags and a laptop bag.

As I got down, I saw two people standing in front of the train's door. One of them was dressed in all white attire and he had a tag in hand clearly mentioning a welcoming note with my name, while the other person was dressed in black & white formals, and he was holding a flower bouquet in his hands.

I waved them; they came running to me wearing a bright smile. The other person handed over the bouquet to me shaking his hands and introducing himself as a Personal Assistant to me, further introduced a uniform person as the driver and he saluted me.

I responded with head nodding gestures.

***

I was taken straight to Hazaribagh, travelling in a car. It seemed so beautiful to be back at home with a bigger ground than ever. The dream of my grandfather, which was seen for my Dad, was getting fulfilled by me and that too from my hometown. Everything on the way was looking very similar to the past one. My heart was pounding several times faster. The enthusiasm had the same value as it remained many years back- *Yes Hometown, I'm coming, and I'm coming.*

By the time, we reached in the city, it was almost dusk. I asked them to drop me down at my home instead of the residential complex provided by the authority; I informed them about my plan to shift there by next day.

***

Everyone at my home was terrifically delighted to receive the gem of their family. My adjective as a gem kept on increasing with the traversing time. Earlier it was the American effect, soon followed by a respectable job of a Professor and then finally the big one. Huh, selfish world, desigNation and bank balance counts. I had become a real big man in their eyes, but this feeling was miles away for me. Things meant nothing without some active consequence to come by. For me, becoming an Architect, Journalist, Professor or even IAS was merely the landmark, what mattered to me was my efficiency as every-one of those.

The first three hours went by customary gift showcasing and weighing ceremony, hoisted by ladies and kids of my family. All of them looked out of the world carrying the costliest gifts as they wondered.

Yet again after so long, family dined together, all the faces had smile owned to their portrait. However, some hidden pain traces often were bulging through their talks.

I went up-stairs after the dinner; my uncle was already walking there through the patch. Tension was crept in his action; I went ahead and started talking with him. In the flow of talk, the problem came up flashing.

"This complete stretch of houses, are to be demolished soon. All five hundred houses will be brought to dusts and pieces, a by-pass road will pass from here, our city is developing Aditya," Uncle explained me sarcastically. He soon turned around and got stationed near the parapet, putting both his arms over it. His vision got stuck at the stretch, which was supposed to be ruined. I felt amazed and goosed listening about the scheme, because a huge non-ending stretch of land lied by the side of the houses, which were supposed to be eliminated.

"What are you saying Uncle? It seems so crazy and weird," I replied with astonishing expressions. This was not fitting to the bottle of my planning and engineering skills, "how the planners are dejecting the idea passing the road through the vacant spaces, when it is available in abundant?"

"Son, this is all about power, money, bribes and corruption. The case will definitely come to you. You will soon learn about the matter very clearly. We tried our best to get real insight of the matter but it never worked," Uncle said wearing a disappointed and lost expression, "It's very late son. You go and sleep now; you have your first day as an IAS tomorrow."

We concluded and went by to sleep. However, the news had dragged sleep miles away from me. I decided to open up the file in detail, not because it was a matter of my house but it was a threat to the noble practice.

***

Before joining at the office, I had thought of starting stride with solving the issues of Education System. But a major matter had just swayed in. I ordered to get all the files regarding the by-pass road plan. It took around a week for me to comprehend the matter completely. It was indeed a corrupt practice going all around.

National Highway Authority of India had commissioned a company to conduct a survey and propose a relative layout for the by-pass road. Just then all the mess started happening, the contactor and the Builder Company issued a survey report considering gps system, no on-field survey reports were shown to NHAI.

I immediately called upon the concerned Land Acquisition Department's officer to get detailed scene of the matter. But he didn't open up much, information was still deficient.

I started personal visits in the affected locality, which came to be very helpful and substantial indeed. Some locals came up with opinion, views and statements. They claimed that surveyors of the builder group came up with a layout tearing the settlement because, if at all it had been through open field then it would have demolished the small plant, which was owned by a local political leader. The story became very crystal clear to me, but for my confirmations, I again called upon the officials and conducted a brain storming meeting. Moreover, partially the truth matched with what was shared by the local people.

However, the freshness and rebellion attitude of mine had no other ways of dealing with the situation. I shared the happenings with uncle and rest of the family members, I suggested them to have a meeting with all affected houses and there owners and file a case against the notion in best possible way. It was indeed an optimist way to grave ways for a beautiful avenue.

Soon a meeting was organized among the natives and affected populace. All of them filed a case against the notion making, NHAI and Abhineel Group, the answerable party. The case was well initiated by my uncle being an advocate. I consulted few planner friends of mine and got drafted a new proposal of the same by-pass road through the vacant patch, which was well supported with estimates of both the proposals, prepared by our end and by NHAI. In every respect, the estimate of our proposal was cheaper than the one drafted by the Abhineel Group, for the matter of fact that their proposal involved more construction cost owing to the extensive compensation to be given.

The filled case had earned its full flow; answerable party was failing to stand upfront and was gradually losing at all ends. In the meantime, Abhineel Group started playing cheapest of their ploy. They lured land Acquisition Department to issue fake notices to the dwellers of 'to be aquatinted' homes, considering the sparse level of awareness among them. Abhineel Group started showing them the greed of reparation through notices, and they promised to provide compensation as early as they withdrew and came to the authority. In any way, Abhineel Group was supposed to get the work done, failing which there payments won't have been issued by the central government.

Alas! The fools responded in the sway of authority.

It's a shear fact, ours is a nation where populace will even run nude for if they are paid millions of rupees.

Few of the petitioners flew to the Land Acquisition Department, seeking to take away compensation and withdraw from case. Very soon, I received the informtion of the situation in action. First of all, I personally called up the petitioners together and explained them the true details of the happenings, I explained them how Abhineel Group was playing the ploy against them to get their budget passed. The meeting proved worthy as they understood the things clearly, though few of them showed lots of resistance in getting my words. Many of them had opinion that getting compensation is there personal choice and nothing or none should try affecting it. However, my persuasion as an officer triumphed over there raw baseless attitude and flanked decision.

Post to that, I called up an official enquiry against officers of Acquisition Department to get proven the result of scam behind by-pass. Gradually all links started opening.

It became very clear that local political leader was the person involved behind the whole scam. Then the homework to generate evidences against him began in full flow, I started following up with call tapings, emails and all correspondences, which had occurred between Acquisition Department, Abhineel Group and the Politician.

The assault was on, but complexions that are more new were set to knock. It came to my notice that Education Minister of the state was charging some money in form of bribe as revert to affiliation to colleges. This was again a big hilarious tone for me. As he was asking bribe merely for signing an affiliation paper, it was clearly reflecting his confines.

That matter was putting many questions on the progress of education in the state. I tried finding my ways to shut down this unpleasant event but it seemed beyond my reach. I tried getting few Professors of concerned colleges in my confidence, and again my words won over them. They agreed to support me; video tapes of such incidences were arranged. I made a mistake of having lots of faith in the central ministry; I forwarded the tape to them expecting an action from top.

On the other hand, Writ Petition filed against the NHAI and Abhineel Group received some un-anticipated consequence. Abhineel Group took hold of Justice of The High Court and the Advocate commissioned in favor of public, which remained ever unknown for all the citizens. The decision given by the honorable court said, "The proposed alignment cannot be altered as it has reached to the stage of 3-D and DPR, any alteration will subject to a big loss to the Central Government. Moreover, also considering the matter of fact that it connects to National progress, petitioners must cooperate with the administration and the Government."

Wow! my honorable Justice, you never even felt an urge to reject a wrong happening just by considering the fact that it will cause things to begin from scratch.

Action often speaks of you and that incidence spoke deep about the legal officials, they were very much buyable.

Two things became very clear to me from then: Laws are made only to safeguard the rights of authority and one should never be sure after building a house in India, authorities might bring it to dust any time at the name of what they call 'Progress and Development'.

I tried talking with the Prime Minister but it all went in vain. I was instructed to not try proving myself as a high breed dog. But, whatever it may be, I was helpless, even my house, an IAS of then, was to be demolished, then where comes the deal of *Mango Man*?

Central Government never took the needed action even against the Education Minister; instead a firing beamer came all over me from there end.

I was transferred to a new city. Ministry didn't find my stay appropriate at my hometown. Being new, I never dared to enquire answers for the same; rather I preferred to flow with the stream.

My hometown had turned bitter for all administering it from the time after my appearance, but they were not ready to feel the adverse taste for long.

❑

10. The lost Patliputra

I had always witnessed that situation, just by hearing and in movies. It happened to me this time as a real-time example. The transfer arrived when I was about to do something good and worthy for the society. It was not the first time when hurdles were in middle of the track, but the teachings of my Father always evoked me to walk ahead with vision to cross over each threshold. Many great swimmers often say–'Best I feel to swim while fighting against stream'.

Fiat stopped in front of the Collector's Office. Though, people claimed Patna being neat and clean under administration of new Chief Minister, I was psychologically primed for the saga district used to be known for many years back.

When I started walking through the lobby, gallery and to the cabinet, I was welcomed by many salutes. After welcoming, introductory formalities followed up. As soon as, it got over, I started darting through the files, which took enough time finally ending up the day by the closing bell. Files didn't contain much complains, it was more floated with 'To Do's' this was indeed a reflectance of the progress song city was on. I had never been to this place for long times, and after I returned from America, the city had a different story to say on a contrast to the experience during my stay, post to matriculation.

That day I was back to home with a very happy note. Pain of transfer was blemished away with the warmth of my companion and successor. On that node, they had accompanied me to my newly commissioned district. It was much easier for Trisha now as Kartik had turned one year old by then.

"How was your first day in new office IAS *sahib*?" Trisha asked making me wear festoon of her arms.

"It had to be good for every sake, this time the first face I saw was of the prettiest lady of my life," I said planting a kiss on her brow, "moreover, the flavor of luck diced into my lap." My hug became tighter. Soon the lovely weeps of my heart's piece started ringing. Trisha ran back to the bedroom, so did I. Kartik was awake. Trisha, clutched him within her adore lured embrace and started feeding him.

"It seems after the arrival of junior *jee*; you have left bothering about me," I said poking Trisha, "what about me?" I winked.

"You got all what you needed," she said and busted into a notorious smile. "Anyways, you freshen up. You must be very hungry. I have cooked *kheer* and *chapati* for you today, your ever favorite."

"Yes, oh…that is wonderful," I said and went.

That evening, I dined with Trisha after long. Sense of completeness was flying high that evening.

"Was there lots of trouble? I was really shocked to get sudden knowledge about your transfer," Trisha asked me putting chapatti into my plate.

"Everything will be fine now. You are by my side now then who can give even a little trouble to me?" I caught her hand, and tried neglecting the issue.

I had started enjoying the beautiful life in the company of my companion and future. However, the true fact is that neither rebels stop nor do the bad scriptures.

I had developed a new concept in city; that concept was against the hidden most corruption of any society. It was widely observed by me that city was populated with numerous coaching institutes and training centers which had indeed become the easiest way to mint money, adopted by numerous science graduates. Forget about just graduates, even the faculties of NIT, Patna were involved in giving coaching for various entrance examinations at a very high cost.

As per the new concept one had to get a license from district authority to establish such an organization. Moreover, even the option of license was not that undemanding, one had to really prove that teaching was the priority over business, and even after receiving the license one had to teach, free of cost, to the economically backward class.

The process of license involved a tough interview, which was to be conducted by an impartial panel, which included me as well. The CM of then never took much time to pass the rule within the city. He had enormous faith in me.

A notice was given to all such coaching institutes after the implementation of the new system at district level. The notice informed them to obtain a license as soon as possible, failing which the Institutes were subject to be crashed into pieces. I never wanted to elongate the scene; the only time provided to them was two weeks.

Issue of notice was soon followed with bribery session in the form of both money and valuable gifts; the determined and *Gandhian* attitude of mine ravished all of them bad for this act of misconduct. I filed an individual case of 'attempt to bribe' against each one of them.

Situation of the city had started turning hot and flamed. I was being held responsible for extinguishing many *chullhas*. Journalists and Media had begun taking much warmth out of it. The things had begun being taken up in other ways. Media had started claiming me an enemy and intimidation to the grooming of Education System and an irresponsible Administrator. However, I never cared and kept marching ahead, because I knew it very well, what I was doing.

Just a day before the end of notice period, I was called upon by the CM of the state. I went to him, with lots of negative things bunched in my laps.

Gateman instructed me to wait until the CM comes. I kept waiting for almost half an hour when finally the CM arrived. I greeted him with a salute. He responded back with an urge to seat.

We both sat on the royal sofa in his office and started conversing.

"Aditya, stop it all immediately before all the things get spoiled," CM instructed me, his voice seemed very imposing and seemed to contain agitation too.

"Sir, there is no way, I can impede it and you too know that it is well justified. We had a strong discussion as well regarding the matter some days ago," I reciprocated.

"Yes, I remember it well. However, the situation doesn't

permit for any more implications, already riots and strikes have started. Both public and media are behind you," CM tried to make me comprehend about the concern.

"Sir, if we back out now, this will reflect our Achilles' heel. Truth will not triumph, evil will get over correct," I tried explaining the CM with full perseverance, "and, I don't worry at all for myself. I will take all woes with both chests open."

"Aditya, there are many other things as well, which are to be taken in to consideration. You know, this agitation may wreck your personal life. You are a family man, isn't?" CM's voice contained threats in them.

"I know how to care for my family, sir. Those weak and cowards can't even dig a hair out. I'm already a transferred Officer, I know how to take up the heat," I replied back, arrogance smelled from my voice.

"It's alright, you will be taking up blows easily, but I don't want any political problems to come by. Opposition can critically use this situation to wreck the existing government both at centre and at state. You will end up taking us all the way out," CM showed his personal concern in the matter.

"It doesn't matter to me sir. I'm a civil servant not a government caretaker. I will do what seems best for administration, might be its obsession and ego but unfortunately, I can't keep it aside," I firmly replied.

"Don't act so smart Mr.IAS, you will be nowhere. Don't get in mess with lion, while living in forest," CM kept threatening me, but it was sure not to alter my intentions.

"I feel pity upon this whole system sir…I won't stop at all. This is the beginning, here I declare, I will further ban Cigarettes, Alcohol, the key business of all industrialists. One must be aware, they can neither sell education nor poison freely," I made firm declarations and stood up to take the leave. That was a gaffe; *intention should never be exposed to the enemy at the gates. These days, wars are fought not by moral code but by politics.*

"Shut up, you ass. Get out from here. You will be destroyed and ravished very soon. I'll show you the power of ministry," CM cried aloud like a mad dog.

I replied back with a smile, "I was already leaving sir, but let me tell you; soon all files will be opened. Might be some files hold your name too?" Finally, I took the leave from him. *It is tough to cover up, once a hole is seen through the barrack and it widens too fast.*

I got out and sat into the car.

"Where are we going now sir? Home?" asked the driver.

"Yes," I replied.

Many thoughts had begun embanking through my nerves. My transfer was obvious along with some acerbic prizes for the time to come, and it was clearly understood, I hardly had a day or two in my hand. I was both worried and heated.

"Take me to the office of Commissioner right now," I instructed the driver. It was six in the evening by then. Clouds were showering full, which had made evening darker than it was.

I reached to the Commissioner and made an instant meeting with him and many other police officials. I had made up my decision, and it was never to be misrepresented. *I know, whatever I was going to do was very wrong to my ethics and sake of humanity but situation wanted this evil at my hands.*

I took a battalion of police, while I got seated along with the Commissioner, SP and DSP in a jeep. A bulldozer accompanied us. The clock read eight. Horde was still alive, though most of them had took an escape from rain staying at home.

The act that happened next still raises my hairs through the body and brings current in my spine. All the coaching institutes, entrance examination centers, non-licensed bars, and alcohol shops were crushed down to earth. People came weeping and pleading to me, but blood was floating high in my eyes.

This was indeed the act of an insane. Some people said that I was an inhuman and I know they were correct.

It was midnight by the time I reached my residence. Trisha was sitting at the entrance steps, waiting for me. Jeep dropped me and left. I walked towards her devastated, she came running towards me. She kissed me several times on my face, followed with several bangs on my chest. Finally, she dragged me towards her, taking hold of my collar and asked, "Why did you do this,

Aditya? You were not of this way." She caught hold of me in a hug and started crying deeply. Her tears kept pouring with the rain. I remained numb, not answering at all through the time.

Media had covered the whole issue and Trisha had witnessed it all. *Situation turns things around.*

This act was followed with my one month deferment and transfer to a place, which all would have hated to be recruited at. I was transferred to Dhanbad, the land of coal.

❑

11. Tasting the coal

The clean record of an honest officer had got its first black medal. I had joined Dhanbad, post to one-month suspension. Since very long, this city had bad image in front of administrators, because of the fact that coal mafias used to administer the city, actually. I had moved carefree around the city but Trisha was not contented with this transfer.

The initial days kept running very smoothly, unaware of the issues to come by. It was for the matter of the fact that, I kept myself away from any unnecessary complexities for some days. However, there are few things and people who never change. It was the case with me as well.

Trisha and I were watching the evening news, silently seated in the drawing room while Kartik was sleeping because of viral fever. My senses got alarmed to see what was being telecasted in the television. It was a report on depleting earth content in Dhanbad and around, because of burning mines within the crust.

"Oh, it is very dangerous. We don't know, which place will slide when!" Trisha showed concern making a frown.

"Hmm, this is a very serious matter. I wonder why government never took note of it earlier. They would have easily minimized the mining practices within the city and could have shifted settlement to some other place," I said.

"But had it been easy enough? Shifting whole city and shutting down the mines? Why won't we use that energy or minerals available in the crust?" Trisha enquired.

"Yes, shifting would have taken time and very tough executions but never so impossible. Indeed it would have been better than dying," I tried explaining the issue to Trisha, "and mines should be shut down because we already have many other mines available in the other parts of our Nation. Moreover, we should always head towards alternative energy dependency rather than on these conventional forms. You understand! all below our earth the crust is burning. It's all gone."

"Don't know, Adi? Moreover, even you should also not think much about it, let's keep living as normal as it could be. Now, I don't want any complications anymore," she replied.

She came close to me and tied me in a hug; I patted on her back and replied with a smiling node. But bug had found its place: my brain.

***

Next day I asked my subordinate to arrange all the reports related to coalmines and the related issues. I started observing and reading them carefully. Too much time passed away, after rigorous effort the whole story became transparent to me. A concrete plan was to be made soon. I started working on it, but never disclosed to Trisha even a bit about it.

This mission was indeed, supposed to be one of the most dangerous activity of my career till then. The involvement of coal mafias was further tightening the scene.

I started up with the normal issues and reforms. Cigarettes and Alcohol were fully banned in the city as a first step towards enforcing law and order in the city. Again, many issues came up concerning employment loss, but I countered them all very well. New employment opportunities were introduced in the system. People were being recruited as neighborhood and society keepers. They were the people held responsible for the improvement and maintenance of the respective locality. Not only this, I had also started up with small-scale schools where unemployed educated people were given employment as teachers. All these small schools were funded by municipality from the funds raised against fines, that was charged from traffic rule violators and many as such.

So, this time I didn't wish to play any insane game as happened in Patna. Strategy was very smooth for me. Prior to any happening the black medal had to be turned white.

Public and media had started appreciating my steps and approaches. Dhanbad was at a snail's pace turning into a well-managed, clean city. However, a sort of cold war was going on between me and few unknown persons.

Banning of alcohol and cigarettes had turned down the large business sector, though small scale employment was provided to many. But how will one flourish with such small scale income, if one has been in a habit to earn gold at the cost of selling poison. I was being asked for the numerous justifications by many authorities.

I had only one message for them, "Banning alcohol and cigarette means no crime. Now no husband is going to shout at his wife for more and more money to full his appetite with ethanol content. This will stop youth from falling on wrong path. Now, no casual sex encounters will occur and even it will tighten bolt against all the crimes thrashing female. No unnecessary street quarrels leading to extreme violence and many as such. There is no point, this step befalls. It is indeed a savior's path."

A step was taken to shut all crimes, but some big crimes against me were waiting.

The big mission was still due. After having observed successful concourse of the ban of alcohol and cigarette, I started up with the next one.

Notices were issued to coalmine owners to evacuate the mines and hand it over to the authority. Many mine owners were among the owners of alcohol retails. Rage was ultimate step by the competent people. All the mine owners came together against the step by the district development authority. They mislead the workers of the mines, organized strikes and campaigns against the authority. They were directly targeting me, which reflected through the slogans they passed on.

The labor community is most fierce when they come into action and they are normally unstoppable. I tried my best to convey the real message by speaking to them amid the rallies and campaigns. The situation was gradually getting out of hands; violence had become the reason for the survival.

The city of coal was burning. Moreover, I being an administrator was unable to rescue it. The picture was very clear to me; if the mines were not cleared, fire would have hit the city badly. Dhanbad would have lost its geographical identity.

***

Few things can't be kept under cover for long; Trisha got the notice of it. She tried her best to stop me to continue with this assault but something else was in my mind. It was not easy for me to get away after being so deeply indulged into it.

Trisha was serving dinner to me but I was very quiet and calm.

"Please put off this mission. You had promised that you won't be ever involved in any litigation, if you remember that situation in Patna?" Trisha reminded me of long back hostile time of Patna.

"I remember it well, but what to do? I'm not an entertainer or something as such so as I will keep watching or frame anything with public's interest. Rather, I need to see their welfare. Moreover, mission is in its high stage, so there is no point to call it off," I said biting chapatti.

"Please try to understand. Those people, to whom you are trying to mess with are very dangerous. What if they…" Trisha started crying without completing her lines.

I tried consoling her with pats on her back. She further said, "I can't take it anymore. No way, I can see even a scare mark either on you or Kartik."

"Calm down, Trisha. Has anything ever happened to us, don't you have faith on me? Everything will be fine and great," I said running my palm through her dense hair.

"I don't know? You have to stop…you have to stop," she left without finishing the dinner.

I felt aggravated and devastated. I never cared to go and share some talks with her. I lied in the drawing room seeking some sleep, which was nowhere to be seen.

***

As perceived by Trisha, issue had begun finding harsh links. I was greeted with stone storms, during a rally. I had been there to make people understand about mines evacuation concerns, but they never thought for a while on the words that I shared.

I took off from there disappointed, disheartened and injured, but I didn't order to blow sticks against them, and after all they were the innocent populace flanked by the mine owners.

Ways were turning dull and blemished; I was unable to see any light ahead. Ministry had started putting its involvement in the issue. I was able to sense hitherto one more transfer with no consequence to the mission taken up.

Yet orders for my transfers had not arrived; only three days remained due for the notice period to get over. As per the experience of last time, I was anticipating transfer orders in a day or two.

❑

12. Love in danger

I was seated with darkness all around. Every pulse was killing a discrete hope. Trisha was upstairs playing with Kartik. We had minimized talks among ourselves since past one week.

No cries, no tears, yet lots of fright were present to accompany me in the dark.

Suddenly, there appeared a sparkle of bright yellow light in front of my eyes, followed with a booming sound. Glass pane of drawing room was there on the floor broken into pieces. I could not react much to the situation, surroundings looked hallucinated all around. Trisha came running downstairs; Kartik was crying deep and was stuck to the mother's lap. Tears were running through her eyes as well, which had turned reddish. I immediately jumped to get both of them in a hug and we pounced to the side of a column.

Panic rolled on through my spine, as I rose up to yell the names of security men. They came in rushing, few of them stayed outside finding the culprits, but no one was seemed visible. Security alarms started buzzing through the vicinity. Soon three more blasts occurred in front of my place of stay. Fortunately, nothing happened to any. All in a while I realized, the blasts were not made to harm me, but were an eye opener warning to me.

She abruptly screamed on me, "I beg your pardon Adi, please for god's sake and for Kartik, stop all these complexities. I want a simple life; I don't have any dream as you have. The only dream, which I hold is a prosperous family, let me live it…let me live it…"

I remained speechless, her pleads had no response from me. I stood stoned, cursing my fate. However, destiny had some other games to play, and I had to be a part of it.

***

The last prevalence had brought great change to my life. Trisha had left me all alone; she had gone to her mother's house without forecasting anything about her return. It had been only a couple of days but difference had started falling high on me. I had been badly addicted to both Kartik and Trisha since last six months, and the moments with big challenges ahead seemed like never ending ages.

I tried making numerous calls to her, but all went in vain. Frustration was turning denser than impenetrable. On the other hand, deadline for notice had reached, authorities had started flushing off and capturing coal mines. The issue didn't remain that simple to be solved at the hand of authorities, the campaigners had started turning violent. They had declared open war against the authority. Many officials were wounded by their assaults.

It had been three days from the notice deadline. Whole Dhanbad was burning in the fire of riots. I was not able to decide with the next decision.

That day, I received a call from the Chief Minister, he asked me to pull down the campaign without thinking much about the related consequence.

I tried my best to convince him, but he had only one say, "No life losses at all. We cannot destroy so many innocent lives at the cost of mistakes, which some cupid brains have done. We will need to get hold of them instead."

"Sir, till then whole Dhanbad will get burnt and you won't be left any place to take action upon," I countered CM's saying. One thing was clear to me; *they will end up this mission for sure*.

"You are not the decision maker. I have decided and you have to call it off. That's it," replied the CM with an imposing tone. "Sir, if this mission is called off, you won't even have anyone alive to vote yet." This was a very outspoken statement that I had made, and I was eagerly waiting for the next line talking about my transfer.

"Don't act very smart, Aditya. We politicians know what vote means and what life of a citizen means. You simply follow the instruction as government's dog," CM vomited worst, whatever he could. I didn't care to reply him and cut the phone back with a sense of disappointment and disrespect.

I instructed my subordinate to pull off the mission. He, very disappointingly, took my order and went ahead.

Had the populace been educated enough, they would have understood what I meant to them through my mission. If education doesn't cover up whole Nation, then no one can postpone or kill the probability ascertaining decline of Nation.

Mission was left unfinished; time was not finding a good pace to run. Every step to be taken filled me with loads of fear of incompleteness. At the juncture of devastation and losses, we often remember our beloveds and it was happening with me too. I didn't had courage to share my pain with my parents either, I was in search of a shoulder to cry upon.

When you miss the one you adore or is ardor to you, then the moments of past start jamming in the cerebrum of yours. It happened with me too.

It was a social networking site where I was promoting my maiden literary work, she added me as a friend considering my uniqueness as an author in Architectural fraternity. She started sending messages and emails, which I ever replied, gradually our cell numbers were exchanged, followed up with many long night calls. We never knew when our relation started taking a shape, for which I even dropped the proposal of joining an MNC as an Architect Journalist. People had often claimed non flourish of relation between us, but they were wrong. We succeeded…but truly did we? Numerous questions started stacking in my brain.

Hunger for votes and non judgmental approach due to the lack of education is making our Nation suffer the most. People conclude with assumptions, they walk on the roads providing momentary pleasure, they fear the force of goodness, but never they back you ever if you take anything up using the force of goodness.

❑

13. City of graduation

My deeds were paying me heavily. Nothing seemed to be running the way, I would have anticipated. The talks of moral education seemed only confined to school textbooks and elders preaching. I was turning as a loser in all respects, no profession seemed suiting me or some can even say, I was not suitable for any profession. I was unable to be a good father, good son and a good husband even.

More goodness you do, more you get drowned in the river. Or might be the definition of goodness needs some conditional captions to be added.

However, hope was still being added to my bucket constantly by my Father. Everything seemed changing, but that great man's visions still remained same, unshaken by the tides around.

I was sitting lonely in my room. My transfer orders had come in, I was transferred to a new city, and it was the city where I graduated from, Cuttack…indeed city of colors. The transfer papers were in front of me pressed by my mobile stationed on the center table, a bottle of rum and a wine glass was kept aside too, I remained in half-drunken state.

It is said- *when nothing goes your way, get drunk and out of senses, at least then pain will be healed for some moments.*

My mobile buzzed, lightening the dark area surrounded momentarily. I peeped in, Dad was making the call. I dragged my hand to pick the phone; it seemed very tough for me as I was partially to my sense. I picked it up, but it fell down because of trembling hand. I bent down and picked it up with firmness, switched it on and made a call back to Dad.

"What happened? Your phone was switched off after the very first call I made. Are all things fine there?" Dad asked me.

"Yes…Dad, great… all is fine. I'm doing as great as an IAS. Your dream has been rewarded," I replied. Words were not easy to come.

"Adi… are you all fine? Is there something wrong, you seem very low…please tell me," Dad asked apprehensively.

"I'm all very great Dad. You tell me how is Mrs.Sinha…? I tried making moments light. Very often, I used to call my Mom as Mrs. Sinha.

"She is very fine. All is magnificent here. But, seems something has gone wrong at your end. However big you become, but you will always remain and be a kid for me being my son. Isn't? Moreover, how are junior Mrs. Sinha and Junior Aditya?" Dad questioned me. His words broke me a tad.

I started crying, "Yes Dad, I'm your son and I don't want to be anything else. I'm not a good Husband, Father and not a good Civil Servant even," I broke into an intense cry. Tears started to flow as a rigorous river.

"Son, don't cry. You kept on hiding everything from us, thinking it will ever remain unknown. But, how can troubles of your path remain anonymous to us for long? And who says you are not a good Husband, Father or a Civil Servant? You are an ideal man. The generation of present era have been hearing tales of *Bapu* and *Netaji*, but you have portrayed there sayings within yourself so well. Cheer up man! We are proud of you," Dad tried encouraging me with his words as usual.

"Yes, Dad…yes…yes. I want to confess something. Please keep it to you, don't tell it to Mom," I said wearing a notorious giggle.

"Hmm...Hmm…go ahead," said Dad.

"I'm drunk today. I swear, I never did it before," I said.

"I had perceived it very early, Adi. I won't tell it to your Mom, but you need to make a promise to me. Will you?" Dad asked me.

"Yes Dad, for sure. Tell me, what do I need to do?" I firmly said Dad.

Dad laughed and said, "Go to Trisha, and bring her back. *Laxmi* should not be away from home for long, she is your Lucky-Charm. Trust me, things will recuperate lost track, once she is back. However, you need to spit of your self-esteem for it, or else I won't take time to spit off your deed."

"Yes sure Dad, you are right and very soon I will find how I can regain my family... By the way I have been transferred to Cuttack and I will be joining there in a couple of days," I said, "and, I'll talk to Mom tomorrow, otherwise she will know it all."

"Oh, so many transfers. Congratulations! Someone is becoming a famous officer. That is a pleasure for you indeed that you are joining in the city, which made you the way you are, that is great news," Dad replied.

"Yes Dad, true. Ok, good night for now, I will talk to both Mrs. Sinha soon. For now, cannot talk with Mom at all, she will get to know," I replied back as the final say.

Dad wished me at last, the goodnight greetings and cut the phone.

That talk had again filled me with lots of enthusiasm and hope. The dream again looked firm and getable to me. I had decided to bring Trisha and Kartik back, and correct one of the biggest mistakes of my life, before it turned into a blunder.

***

I had landed up in the silver city, the conurbation of my graduation. The city had witnessed lots of changes since last half decade but one thing seemed so common, the spiritual colors still prevailed. I had first time witnessed this color of Cuttack during my graduation, the city witnesses almost three hundred and sixty five festivals in a year. Flowers, cow dung, vermillion and many.

I had widely observed city during my five-year stay for my graduation. I even then had enormous respect for their ultimate faith and belief on God. One can easily find a temple after every half a kilometer, so many festive processions and rallies. The city is beautifully sandwiched between two rivers, Kathajori and Mahanadi with so many narrow lanes running through the city.

However, one thing I never liked about the city was- few people of street never used to respect any girl and always saw them with courteous eyes. A beauty, damsel always seemed matter of feast to those filthy robust eyes. Public often were allowed to get drunk openly by the street, the number of temple was almost equivalent to the number of alcohol selling shops.

Getting a perfect loop free hand is always a task similar like reaching an Everest. But by then, I had become habituated to draw circles with all necessary instruments.

I joined office just next day from my influx. As usual, I received a very warm welcome. I knew it well, I was only few days guest at every office, and it hardly takes some time to lob me away.

The work had begun extensively in a customary tone. The stir again occurred with proscription of cigarettes and alcohol in the city. As expected, a strong resistance started coming up against the notion. The city was still the same with regards to edifying and physiological values. No one was ready to accept the change at straight hands. This time, the Chief Minister promised me for a support to full coverage. This was rarest of occurrence and thereby it was a big welcoming gift to me.

People started organizing campaigns, rallies and district level strikes against the notion, but ministry's support didn't let trouble occur for long. The notion was implemented by full force. Some threatening calls started arriving on my number, but I never panicked and acted nattily to the state of affairs. Making indispensable arrangements, I tapped the numbers and butchery action was taken against countless of them. The firm determiNation and boosting words by Dad had made me stronger and resilient towards the life. All the time the dialogue by Rajesh Khanna in the movie 'Anand' kept me going for more and more, '*Babumoshaye, jindagi lambi nahi badi honi chahiye' (Brother, life should be big not long)*.

After long, things seemed to be rolling all with me. Anyway, empathy always looks for more and new. I was also resolute to make life safer and reluctant for females in the city.

Life of traffic police had become tougher and tight from then. Policemen were assigned bike-patrolling duties in non-uniform dresses. They were scattered in various pockets of Cuttack to observe activities minutely. Ratio of police to public was carefully designated bearing in mind demographical statistics. Restaurants, shopping streets, street food zones, theatres, colleges, squares, housing zone squares, all were covered. Moreover, to my perfectness in predictions and analysis, more than hundred cases were reported in span of a week. The defaulters were humiliated or put under bars as per the level of complication. No one was spared *whoever he may be*.

I was very happy for a point that I was correcting all what seemed erroneous to me during my college days, so indeed dream was shaping into an execution. However, Trisha's and Kartik's absence was making me snob some moments every day around. But, all attempts to call her back were failing.

***

Very often, I used to surpass by my college, but I never made my presence there. It had been almost more than a month when I came to Cuttack but the hectic schedules never let me visit it even. I tried calling Prof. Shubhrat on his old number, but nothing seemed effective. Somehow, I managed to get in contact with Ranveer Singh, my batch-mate through a social networking site. He was very happy to know about my arrival in the city. I was equally happy to know that, he was still in Cuttack. We shared our current contact numbers; I immediately made a call to him.

"It has been very long mate. No contacts since your marriage. How is *bhabhi jee*?" Ranveer said following a giggle.

"Yes Ranveer, it has been very long mate. Trisha is very fine, brother. You tell me, how is the whole lot in succession?" I asked, trying to change the topic.

"I'm very tight. My projects are running in flow, very soon I will be launching my own housing scheme…leave mine. My projects are running but I know I stand nowhere to talk about Architecture with you. What are you doing here in Cuttack? You were working as Professor in some college at Nagpur, right?" Ranveer replied.

I laughed and alleged, "Friend, I have waved goodbye long back to Architecture."

"Oh, my god! I can't deem you saying this," Ranveer said wearing lots of inquisitiveness.

"Yes mate. Destiny…destiny…desire…you never know," I replied smilingly.

"Oh, is it? So what did this bird destiny do with you?" asked Ranveer. He was till then unaware of my latest venture.

“I have to come to your city after being appointed as DC, a month back,” I replied him back.

“Oh…oh…so, you are the bloody ass, responsible behind scarcity of my tonic,”

I giggled long in reply.

“Friend, unknowingly I slanged you like hell,” he started laughing again, “but, really feeling pompous for what you are doing. This is an ultimate pleasure to be buddy of an IAS officer. Let’s meet up mate, do spare some time for me poor.”

I laughed long and said, “Sure mate. Let’s go to college tomorrow, I tried calling Prof. Shubhrat several times, but it seems his number has changed.”

“Ok, then done. We will go to college tomorrow for sure, if you are able to find little time from the airtight schedule of yours,” Ranveer replied.

We ended up the call after a long duration conversation, which occurred after a giant gap of time. It was a matter of extreme delight for me to chit chat with a college pal. I made a call to my assistant to canceal all the meetings and appointments following next day, owing to the thought about visit to the college along with Ranveer.

***

I myself drove car to the college next day. I parked the car in the parking lot and made a call to Ranveer. He replied informing me to wait for another five minutes, as he was stuck in a traffic jam.

Ranveer came up near the parking lot; he parked the car near mine. I recognized him easily and got out of the car, his lips spread wide looking at me. We pounced towards each other, and got into a hug. The emotions of then were beyond any lexis. I could never know his emotions but expressions reflected the bouquet of happiness, he seemed to have owned. But for me, emotions were full of contentment; I was with someone whom, I knew from many years. I was with someone with whom, I grew from a teenager to a matured responsible man, I was with someone whom, I had at times been quarrels with; I was with someone by whom a piece of appreciation used to make my day at times.

❑

We entered in the college building; spaces seemed so familier and recognizable. Honestly, nothing much had distorted there. The same red colored bricks, same lush green campus all around, the same gigantic plinth to rise upon, the same monumental podium sprawling all together. The work environment was still the same; students were spread in various pockets with drawing boards, sketchpads. Going ahead, I found few students hiding below the staircase, waiting for the Professor to pass by from there. I could recollect my college days, how we bunked classes and waited in the similar fashion for the Professor to pass by. Ah…again, I wanted to go back to the college, the glorious moments!

We walked towards the office, staffs seemed to be changed, and even the principal was not the same. I was pissed to collect the anonymity in so many recognizable spaces. Hoping for the director to be the same, we enquired the attendant assigned in front of the Director's chamber, but more disenchantment was added to our taste, when he replied, "Bihari sir retired long back, now his Son-in-law is the Director." Both of us looked at each other's face in a sign of grief.

"Is there any old faculty present in the college?" I asked the attendant.

"Yes, Shubhrat sir is there. You can find him on the first floor. But by the way, who you both are?" asked the attendant.

"We are old students of this college, we used to study here, some ten years back," Ranveer smilingly replied to the attendant.

"Oh, old student…good, good, then come and meet with Director Sir, he will be free soon," attendant replied.

"We will come in a while, we can't wait so long," Ranveer replied and hinted me to walk along to the first floor.

"After knowing your identity, he could have send us and dragged us inside calling-Dad, Dad," Ranveer said while passing through the staircase.

I just cared to smile at his words. We walked towards Prof. Shubhrat's old chamber, but we couldn't find him there. Only few old Professors were sitting there, they easily recognized both of us, greeted and received us very happily. They were the one who had joined college during our final year. They were much glad to see both of us together in the campus. Ranveer tried telling them about my identity as an IAS, but I hinted him not to do so and he didn't. I wanted to remain as a normal student to them as ever. One of the Professors hinted us towards the chamber of Head of the Department, when we asked for Prof. Shubhrat. We enthusiastically moved towards the HOD's cabin, both of ours eyes got into a fix what was written there. Prof. Shubhrat had become HOD of the institute.

We both entered into the cabin. Prof. as usual was stuck to the desktop, working out some design's model. He soon turned towards us; he was terrifically surprised and happy to find both of us in front of him. For the moment, he forgot all the things around, he pounced towards us and took us in a deep hug. The emotional pearls found their way through our eyes. Prof. Shubhrat had witnessed lots of change; his eyes were now ornamented with thick lens of beholding and yelling out his experience well coordinated by the grey hair.

We sat there in his cabin for some times, after that we moved out to our old think tank place, the edge of Kathajori river, just in front of college. I narrated him and Ranveer my whole journey till then. Both of them were by the same token excited to hear it. However, it was a true pleasure for me to tell that person about the acclamation, whose path was shown to me by him.

We sat there chit chatting long hours. In the evening, I left from there saying see-off to both, with the promise to meet again. Unfortunately, I couldn't keep my promise to either of them.

❑

14. Second farewell

My old observation was all set to speak up many new things. After numerous interrelations, I had concluded that building religious shrine is best way to bury down one's black money. Also, never we get to know, where exactly the donated money goes to, who knows, we have been dreaming to reach the golden gate of the heaven at the cost of money donated but that donated money after all could never be used better than increasing little more fat to the temple owner. *Who knows?*

The usual bad habit was yet again set to create annoyance to my love. I collected all reports related to the statistics of the existing temples in the city. The figures that I received, justified my sayings; it was almost like a temple per half the kilometers. I don't know, how it never mattered to them, but it was a matter of real disgrace for me to almost get my feet touch, the almighty's platform while having a walk by the side.

But, never that deliberation of fiscal issue ever bugged me before. That concern and my actions to follow up were sure to raise sentimental violence ahead but neither was possible to be bolted, nor that violence nor Aditya Sinha.

I appointed few officials to screen through the monetary offerings at various temples, with varying shifts at different patches. The process continued for some weeks. In the meantime, it was also observed, there were few temples that had started coming up as new structures, one thing was common that most of them were personally owned ones.

Very soon screening results came up, the amount being donated at the temples on particular days like Saturdays and Tuesdays were hell lot more than what a young professional earns in a year. I was amazed to receive this inflated upshot.

Some concerned officials also claimed of some hidden treasury captivators, to hide more money in black. The picture was turning clear and transparent to me.

Cuttack is a place with lots of trade units, this is a kind of centre of export and import, considering the fact that Pradeep Port is nearby, and also it is silver city. Although, Orissa is known among poorest of the states, but the sad fact is, more than poor dwellers, cities are habited by high earning class, with many who never showcase the earned property and keep hiding them in the temples. What if whole amount gets equally distributed among the called poor; might be then so many concerns can be solved. Education, the prior parameter to gain development will come by their hands and the country will progress ahead, which unfortunately cannot happen without money.

In past, there had been numerous instances of income tax raids, but normally they all resulted in failures. Nevertheless, present of then was set to witness a daring history.

I wrote a letter to Intelligence-Bureau regarding the issue involved, but they scattered all my hopes by responding a letter of negligence, claiming no action without approval of the central government. However, every new toy brings bundles of edginess in a kid. Healing the truth and claiming the lost justice to the National interest was like a toy to me, and I was only one-year-old kid in the field. I couldn't behold my patience and I myself commissioned a team of thirty five officers from various departments, who were supposed to take up raids in various temples.

Necessary arrangements were made from a day before the raid; to take care of any riots which, in any case, erupted due to the sentimental evoking. Everything started happening strategically. Five teams were split in various zones, to carry on with the actions. Exactly at the time of closing of every temple, officials took over from the back door. Full resistance came up at the hands of Priests and few devotees who were till then present there. Finally, before anyone could understand anything in details, huge amount of money, gold bats and ornaments were recovered from hidden pits.

Before the final action could come up, news was spread like a fire throughout the city. Despite several measures taken, mob came out on roads, streets and lanes shouting at the name of almighty. The mob was very fierce; they started destroying the government and unrestricted properties. The forces counter covered the attack by the mob, but still they harmed many officials and countless public properties. All the commissioning team, tried their best to escape out from the temples they were in, but two of them were badly trapped by the mob. Unfortunately, we couldn't save three officers; they were ravished very badly while many were indignant badly, the situation had turned hostile. But soon the force was able to take complete command of the situation, many hooligans were dragged into the jail, various got injured, fortunately no life was lost at their ends. It was almost midnight when peace prevailed all around, but something more was sure to come up next morning.

It was indeed a cocktailed evening for me, mission had achieved the completeness, it was all done to the level of perfection but few lives were lost at authority's edge.

I was seated in the drawing room supported at my knees; I was looking deep into the mirror. My throat and pulse were lumping briskly; tears were coming through the eyes, though I was not crying.

Money can be obtained someday or other, money is either the piece of metal or piece of paper, which always has some units to rate. How will I obtain the lost life again, and even will I be ever able to rate the lives gone by? We never came in with money pouched in the belly, and even when we die, it won't come accentuated with us either, then why we the bloody humans are so accentuated towards it? Great was the barter system, where people used to get basic needs at the cost of work they did, no one was rich or poor by birth or malpractice, it was the work which spoke. Currency the bugger...but when I think about other side of the coin, then the thought says, why did you accumulate so much never needed amount of money, that too at the name of almighty? When people came ahead to rescue the money to their respective owners then why did those owners came running to kill those rescuers at the name of same almighty's disrespect? Then where are you still sleeping Almighty? You are so great, why do you want your name being adulterated for so many cheap deeds?

Various thoughts came ramping through my medulla that day, which I couldn't take up more. I dashed my hand into the mirror, and it broke into various microns in one say. A stream of blood flushed out through my palm. Listening to the noise, caretaker came running to me.

"Oh, son, what have you done to yourself? Wait…I'm just coming with some ointments and bandages.

I remained seated and stoned without any reply. The caretaker rushed somewhere and brought up a mug of water, a candle, a cotton cloth, an antiseptic cream and a bandage. He soon treated my hand with his indigenous slant.

"Ok, uncle. Now you go and have a sleep, everything is fine now," I said.

"Yes son, I'm going, but you please take care of yourself. I have seen many IAS officers, but not as crazy as you," caretaker left giving the final say.

***

Caretaker was very correct. I was doing something, which was never expected from an IAS officer, and indigestion was soon to occur in the stomach of high command. It took not more than a day for the things to happen. Next cockcrow brought up news of various reports on hidden black money in the depth of temples through print and electronic media, and I was again transferred to a new city. The scene seemed very hilarious, I was being dismissed for some good job done, and this was accepted by everyone this time as the report said. But, destiny wanted me to script some more good things on the street-pads of some other cities.

I was for the second time receiving farewell from the same place, but both the time on contrasting scenario.

The condition of Cuttack improvised to great heights post to those effects.

❑

15. Fast shifting

For next interval, I received as much as five transfers, I don't know exactly but it might be a record for any IAS officer. It had been almost one and a half year all alone; Trisha and Kartik were not there with me. I was unable to take the pain; the rebel in me had begun dying.

Isolation and severance are deadliest punishment for any, you leave a dog, and even he can't take up its pain. A pet parrot also seeks your company for breathing long.

Though a crowd was always walking with me, with so many adverse colors of traditions, but they only portrayed to be walking beside, no one ever shared the hues as one's companion does. Life partner's shade had vanished from my color wheel and it was hurting a lot by then.

When the horse is running in its best form, we often forget about the pressure and tiredness, he would be getting loaded with, which many times results in breaks to his breath.

I was doing great as an administrator and officer, and it was the time when my best form had just clicked in. But, human always remains a selfish being; I started counting the bullets of happiness, sorrow, success, defeats, gains and losses during the tenure of my best form and very melodiously pessimism won the listing. The selfish human decided to cover up the misses and verdicts was made.

I took up a big decision, a career-churning mug of coffee. I was set to get back to my old passion to stay with my love and ardor forever. The person losing love only knows the taunting hurt-coated gap it sways, and I badly needed my charm back in my life.

It may seem insane and crazy, out of box take to many populaces, but whatever it may be, it happened and I scripted the legend as it appears today.

I sent her a sms informing about my decision. She instantaneously called me back.

"Yes dear, finally I want to leave everything behind. I don't want more than just a simple life with you and Kartik," I said with a little sob.

"You have delighted me a lot Adi, this is the best call of my life. I love you dear…I love you," she replied back.

"I love you too dear. I love you too…please come soon; I can't take it anymore. We will stay in Hazaribagh and practice Architecture again," I said with a sob to accompany.

She also started to cry, she further added, "Yes sweetheart. We will, we will earn less but live happily ever. You know Kartik has begun walking fluently now," she started explaining happily, "but he can't speak properly till now."

"Oh my god! I wish to see him soon, I will do it online… just can't hold on, please bring him upfront as soon as you can," I said impatiently. The emotions were same as it used to be five years back, when I had first met Trisha and we used to do video chats to see each other live.

"Yes, will be there in an hour. You know what; he walks in similar fashion as you walk by making hops," Trisha broke into a laugh while explaining his walking style resembling as that of mine. Even, I replied back with a long chuckle.

We kept talking and sharing moments for some couple of hours. That talk seemed almost honey pourer as the openers of love relation.

***

It was just within a score of days, that it all happened. I gave up my desigNation and had reopened my firm with my life partner. We had started practicing Architecture yet again. Earnings had turned dawdling and challenges had taken up other form but both of us were happy eating the chapatti of peaceful happiness.

This was indeed the fastest shift of my life traversed so far.

❑

16. The Constitution's call

The vivid journey, full of varying experiences and resilient attitude, had won enough laureates for me. I had become an important public figure and very popular among youth. Transfers and phenomenal fire were indeed need of the icon they wished to have. Apart from youth, some others too seemed having it in there trot too.

I had again got some reasons to live. Trisha and Kartik were coming out to be immense liniment for the scares and wounds achieved during my past tenures.

Trisha and I were enjoying morning coffee of the winters together while Kartik was busy playing with his building blocks.

"Are you sure about the decision?"asked Trisha.

"Yeah, I'm very confirmed about it. See Trisha, I always had dream of culminating the errors existing within system of ours. If there is an opportunity, then why to let it go? I have realized it well enough, nothing can be turned to even a minute angle until torque results from an eminent power," I described and took bite of toast.

"But, do you feel that, Dad will agree upon what you are doing? And even if we forget about what Dad and Mom think, don't you think the prosperity of our family will be again lost somewhere?" Trisha said making a frown.

"See, right now Dad and Mom, both are not present in town. And irrespective of what they will say, I want to conclude straight away. Though I know, Dad will never deny, I will never take any chance for National benefit," I explained while trying to convince her, "Also you had made the promise to ever support me achieving all endeavors I eye for."

“That I will do for sure whatever the consequence might be, provided prosperity and peace prevails in our life,” she said placing her hand over my fist.

Kartik had erected a building’s model in the lawn, Trisha and I smiled looking at each other.

Being parent is always a matter of big pride and happiness, but why administrators and authorities don't realize that they are the guardian of all they are administering? Care for public and their welfare along with National, global progress must be their sole aim. Alas! They never realize.

I was firm with my apparition. General Lok Sabha elections were to fall in within due course of quarter years and I had been given ticket by Indian Public Alliance, then the party in opposition. It was well known to me, no political party does work for the social benefits. The real agenda is always to increase transactions in hidden bank accounts and they wished me in party only to lure a constituency seat and to get to the seat of central supreme. It had been a history of long when they were able to win through that constituency; party was determined to break its jinx.

Party President of IPA knew me well enough; I had first met him during my tenure as an IAS at Dhanbad. He had shown bundles of support towards my actions for shunting of coalmines, which also followed my campaign at Cuttack and more. I ever believed his support as an act of goodness and that had left me with an honest image of him. It is said, appearance and personality speak most of you until spoken. He was a man in mid forties, most often he wore white outfit in form of *Kurta*, *Pyjama* or Prince Suite at times, which appealed a lot about his modesty and intellectuality.

There was a time when I was a big adherent of this party, then I was a school kid and sayings of elders dominated my thoughts.

At many times, I supposed many changes are needed through the whole set of system. Even The Constitution we follow doesn’t fit into the context of now. My analysis and considerations have given me reasons for its wastefulness.

***

It was the time when, country was all set to receive

independence. The quest to become prime Minister was alarmingly forcing in so many things. We needed a constitution to declare India a republic. Hostile was the situation, as riots at the cost of partition had wrecked India badly. If one clearly peeps into the history, our constitution holds, things will become very apparent to him.

The process of fruition of Constitution began much earlier than 1947. Its origin is closely related to India's struggle for independence from British rule. Way back in 1885 the leaders of India's freedom struggle put forward a document called Constitution of India Bill, which envisaged freedom of expression and equality before law. In February 1924, Motilal Nehru introduced and passed a decree outlining the procedure for drafting and adopting a Constitution for India in the Central Legislative Assembly. In 1927, Lord Birkenhead, the Secretary of State challenged Indian leaders to produce a Constitution which carries behind it, a fair measure of general agreement among different sections'.

The INC accepted the challenge and convened an All Parties' Conference in 1928, which appointed a committee under the chairmanship of Motilal Nehru to determine the principles of Constitution for India. The Nehru report submitted on 10th August 1928 was in effect as an outline of a draft Constitution of India. It confirmed equal rights to men and women regardless of caste, class, religion or region, free elementary education, freedom of expression to all etc. The secular character of the state was listed as fundamental right.

The revolutionary idea that framing of Constitution should be made by a Constituent Assembly elected with widest possible franchise first propounded by M.N.Roy and Jawaharlal Nehru began to gain ground. Congress included it in the election manifesto for 1936-37 elections to provincial legislatures. The British agreed to it only in 1945 after the end of Second World War. As an election based on universal adult franchise will require lot of preparations and will take lot of time. Congress had to agree to the cabinet mission's scheme of elected provincial assembly members electing the members of Constituent Assembly. Congress won a huge majority of seats in the Constituent Assembly. The Congress working committee made great effort to see the members from scheduled Caste and Tribes, Women, Christian, Parsis and Anglo-Indians were among the Congress Candidates. There was also an effort to bring in best available talent whatever be the political affiliations. Thus 30 members, who were elected on Congress ticket, were not its members. The Muslim League continued to oppose the Constituent Assembly raising the demand for a separate State. Even though it won a big majority of Muslim seats, it never took part in deliberations of the Assembly.

The first session of Constituent Assembly was held on December 9, 1946 and was attended by 207 members. Dr. Rajendra Prasad was elected as Chairman. The Assembly formed different sub-committees dealing with different aspects of the Constitution. The most important Drafting committee was under the chairmanship of Dr.B.R.Ambedkar. After long and painstaking deliberations and several modifications lasting for 166 days in a period of about three years the Constituent Assembly approved the draft Constitution on November 26, 1949. The longest written constitution became law on January 26, 1950.

There were no major problems in that time, like those which our country is facing today; the parameter of technological advancement has out-done the biggest Constitution of World. Neither had we had any other option for the same; so that a comparative analysis would have given us a chance to look at the best. Another worst reason behind it is that youth of now is rarely interested to bring some accentuation towards the same. We will definitely get to know a shameful stat indentifying population being aware about inscriptions within it.

How can one be a good citizen of Nation without knowing its constitution?

And the eagerness to put it in at an earliest also contributed to the failure, which stands today and I was determined to rectify the mistake of past.

***

Campaign for election was in full swing as only a couple of months remained due for the biggest festival of the country. I had a hectic schedule for the same, so many meetings, addresses and phone calls. Party president was very certain for my victory and I was also sure for his misconceptions about my agenda, indeed they were not to be confined only to speeches and papers. I was determined to execute it with full force.

I was addressing public at St. Columba's College ground, "I will revive the Constitution; focus will be lying on eradicating the prevailing loop holes. At many times it is felt, laws are nomadic and hilarious in nature, they lack proper reasoning and logic. Law has to be reinforced in a way that root cause of crime is uprooted henceforth no further need of assaults. The thought running behind them should be- *Why do we need a Jail? What if instead of building jails, we create opportunities for education, which will make people stay away from crimes?* Current edification system will be replaced by better one. I will try my best to convert Agriculture into profession…Nation has befallen at our hands; we will not let it get blemished. Again India will become the Golden Bird. *Jai Hind*!" The speech was appreciated with massive roars and thousands of claps. The environment around was very enchanting and encouraging. I looked into the crowd and waved my hands in return. This was my first vocalizations, which had initiated in an edgy tone but ended with a roar.

"Aditya, you have become an expert at delivering. Really, you touched the soul. Whole public is a lollipop sucker, keep supplying lollipops and they won't even ever look for if flavor was ester made, not natural," said Rajkamal Awasthi, the party president sharing a giggle to follow.

I replied with a smile, I preferred not saying a petite even.

Power makes change happen; I needed it by hook or crook.

Party had become very hopeful from my attributes and progress in the field. But my hopes and intentions were never intersecting in reality. I was eying for the Nation's call and the call by the Constitution, the young lad of Hazaribagh, who once wanted to be an Army man, was trying to fulfill his buried desire to full.

I returned home from the party rally. Dad was eagerly waiting for me, while Trisha and Mummy had gone to market for some shopping pre to '*Teez puja*' celebration.

"How are the proceedings so far?" asked Dad, while his head was dug into the newspaper being seated on his ever-favorite rocking chair, placed within the lawn. Ambience was just very perfect; two light posts were illuminating the reading zone with enough radiance. The pouring white light was bifurcating the beautiful fresh night, forming show of glittering triangle. The especially designed study zone was well surrounded by bright green low heighted hedges while corner was addressed by *lovely Red Lal Bahadur Shashtri roses*. Those roses depicted my grandfather who was very fond of red roses. He used to pin it to his court every morning…ah…memories…memories.

"It was tremendous Dad. I loved addressing public and the matter of the fact is that they loved what I was saying. Moreover, after I received the huge applause, which reinforced ideas become determined milestone to be achieved and there were so many things Dad, which I am really unable to express. Rest all is running good as well, party people are very happy with my work so far." I replied to Dad.

"I don't know Adi, whether I should be proud, or I should feel having lost something. But, I too sense very delighted; now you are fulfilling all dreams what your grandfather had seen. You became an honest IAS and now you are one of the public figures. Country has started knowing you for practice of humanism and Nationality," Dad said raising his head. Sense of proud reflected in the tone he spoke. He soon stood up, placing newspaper on the chair and patted me on my shoulder. I felt overwhelmed and expression of conquer appeared on me.

The struggle had begun. Path always seems very beautiful once the vehicle starts with a smooth tone, even though the fact of bumpy roads ahead is known.

Everyone was playing own styled prank to find solid foundation in politics, few were looking to add more levels while I was planning the chess board game with moves, which would make Mother India smile yet again.

Politics is the art of playing ploys to make a state run, not the disgraceful conspiracy to fill own stomach beyond throat.

❑

17. Reaching the house

I was desperately waiting for the election results to come in as a contrast to the Civil Service exam results. It was true; I wanted to get the chair but not for the reasons as politicians had been doing. Might be, I was yanked towards bright dawn of the next day, till then, which was painted in my canvas of imagiNation. But whatever, once a taste of power is dropped in your maw, you begin tending to accumulate more there.

"I'm little too upbeat for me, reaching the house. I won't be able to overcome if at all dart hits wrong," I said. Trisha listened to me patiently, while going through design of a small residence, through the sketchpad. All the lights were off; accept the side lamp and Kartik was sleeping amid us.

She raised her head, looked towards me, caressed my hair, removed my spectacles and said, "I'm sure that you will get through this fixture. But, I'm apprehensive for the fact, that it is dangerous. It may ruin many," a frown appeared on her face followed with a small snob.

"Indeed life is not certain, death is ultimate truth followed with birth, so why not make life meaningful with aspirations and…" Trisha stopped my verse by putting her palm on my lips and making a pessimistic node.

"Never say this again, never, never…" she said, shining pearls appeared in her eyes. I smiled, brushed her cheek through eyes and hugged her tight while Kartik still remained in middle.

***

Time ran at a great pace as usual, we couldn't notice when the verdict day arrived. All the leaders of various political parties were all jamming up the space at the office of Deputy Commissioner, where counting was being processed, only the leader missing was me. Ah…once, I used to be office bearer there, time had changed.

The sun was now located in middle of southwest and west; the temperature meter was reading the highest for the season. Hazaribagh was burning in the heat, both for the recent speedy deforestation and the climate of democratic festival, although I was in state of extreme serenity.

However where do you get tranquility in this world of havoc, some or other buzz and chrome always exists to wreck your peaceful sleep. And there it was, my phone buzzed, display showed- *Rajkamal Awasthi calling*. I answered the call, "Yes sir, what happened?"

"Are you nut Aditya? Counting is going on and you are absent from here. Just come over here as soon as possible," He was on fire. I felt like laughing, for the situation. What a contestant has to do with the counting? Why can't we wait for the concerned persons to do their job and respect the upcoming consequence? But he was senior to me and due respect was extremely needed as I had to be the part of his system itself. I replied on a submissive tone.

"I'm sorry sir. I will be there in just few minutes," I replied and rushed to my car. The car was there in my service from the party end, for so many reasons, which were never justified to me. The moment I reached, my phone again buzzed while few people sprang outside the office floating powdered colors and vermillion in air. Further, what I saw was unbelievable for me. The Almighty was pouring his blessings and best wishes in full flow, the first step towards conspired dream was accomplished.

The dancing and celebrating swarm carried many party flags, pictogram tags and images portraying me and Rajkamal Awasthi. Many of them soon reached near my car and opened the door. Few fell on my feet while few tried shaking hands with me. I came out but I was unable to react with thoughtful thinking. All happened very fast. One of those from the natives took me up above on his shoulder, and rested in a jeep, which was supposed to begin with a public salutation rally.

"Long live Aditya Sinha! Long live Indian Public Alliance!" So many yells kept covering party and my name. I stood there in the jeep, with folded hands. Many marigold garlands were overweighing my esophagus while my white shirt had turned red, green and blue at many patches. I remained stationed with my initiated posture, as the nervousness was overdoing on me. Crowd kept waving me while few kept trying to find my touch, I felt reciprocating but could not ever try for that.

Smiling and happy heads all around, with massive yell were gradually adding the level of confidence. The jeep kept moving ahead through NH-100 heading towards my own locality. It was a scene of rarity, children, ladies and people from their houses were ravishing out to greet and salute me, in similar fashion how it used to happen many decades ago. I never adored any politician, but this time Gandhi cap was earning some due respect; happy precision was that the person behind it, was me. By the time the rally reached near my own home, the universal almighty was all set to shut down his office, as clock showed two hands were positioned orthogonally and in the direction of gravity. The February waft was chilling it bit too much around ears and nose as vermillion was showing its effect.

Rally was soon over with so many applauses and roars. For the first time in my life, I was able to feel my name annoying me. Those applauding voices and screams were deficiently fluttering within my nerves. I was seeking a sound slumber but how was it possible? Life had different engagements from there on.

"Where are you going after such a hectic timetable? Today, it is a remarkable evening. You should spend some time with your family. Dad will feel bad, when he doesn't find you home after his return from Aunt's abode," Trisha said, as I was set to leave putting on the top most button of the prince coat.

I smiled, turned around, put both my hands on Trisha's shoulder, and said, "Party supreme has thrown revelry for triumphal celebration, and being negligent straight from the first day will be very awkward. Isn't?"

"Your talks are always very smart to leave me speechless all the time. I don't know? I just don't want to let you go today… always you should not be the one to win," saying this she cuddled into my arm and crushed me in her tight hug. I partially separated her, kissed her on her brow and said, "I will have to go dear. You please spare some time with Kartik till then, he too needs to get good education and preaching and you are indeed maximally responsible." I smiled.

She made a frown and left from there.

"Trisha!" I called.

She turned around and threw a mesmerizing smile, floated a kiss and said, "Ok, go and get back soon."

I left from home, while exiting from main gate; my path got interlaced with Dad and Mom. I sprang out opening the gate, Dad offered a smile. I dropped down to touch feet of reasons behind my being, they raised me and hugged me and said, "You have made us proud. Once, I had a feeling you should never be part of this system in this way, but today my thoughts have alterations. Go ahead."

"It's indeed because of your blessings Mom and Dad," I said.

"This is your enormity *beta*, and this makes you so different from many of your generation. But always keep your sense organs at an alert, world is not safe for following imprint of the leaders of yesterday," Mom said. I ended the conversation with a smiling node and left.

"Brother please put FM on," I said to the driver. Car started moving slowly on the deep-dark Hazaribagh road. The background was ornamented with song, *"Jab zero diya mere bharat ne, duniya ko tab ginti aayi…"* and it drove me back to my childhood when Dad used to make me sing these patriotic and socially relevant songs, really how patriotic and Nationalist I was even being so naïve? How beautiful was the moment to go to nearby mosque each day and church every Sunday, and really I enjoyed chanting, reciting and listening the Vedic hymns too. Also every morning, I used to wake up early only to salute the BSF men, who used to pass through the frontage of my house, as we had a BSF camp nearby. Those soldiers recognized me well; few knew my names as well, once I was also carried to their parade on 15th August.

"Kirr…." there was a sudden break of car. Few people had popped near the gate, they were correspondents. I came out, and started answering their questions till before someone came in and informed me to leave from there as soon as possible to reach inside the hall, where party function was going on. I felt bad and was touched to leave having them unanswered and disrespected.

All must be respected, irrespective of job they are doing, may be of administration, teaching, studying, journalism or even sanitary services. One call of disrespect by us, can assure many in days to follow.

By the time I got into the banquet hall, so many known figures were already present by then. I was loaded with few bouquets and flower garland just in due course of seconds, it was so indifferent for me and I was unable to react henceforth. After I moved ahead, Rajkamal Awasthi came near to me, and greeted, "Congratulations young man! Miles to go." He was holding a glass of some blackish red colored liquor. "Hey come here, give a glass to our guest of honor," he said calling one of the waiters.

Soon maître d' came with a tray utterly stacked with glasses filled with reddish black liquors.

"Sorry, I don't drink. If administrator himself is dancing getting oozed by halluciNation controlled by liquid, what will public do then?" I replied wearing a sarcastic smile. Rajkamal Awasthi didn't say anything, he stayed numb for a while, it seemed he had sensed the radicalism hidden in me.

"Why did you become so numb, sir? I was just making moment light. Actually, I have taken resolution not to drink, till our party reaches till the level of zenith. You only tell how can I break it?" I replied, yet again smiling sarcastically.

Politics must be for the good cause, Lord Krishna had said- The lie spoken for the benefit of mass is better than a truth, which ravishes and wrecks through numerous lives.

Throughout the function, I interacted with many new faces and people, all were deeply interested to know about unique voyage and transformations of mine. Indeed, I was then a political leader who was once an Architect, Journalist, Professor and an IAS.

When I reached home, light was still glittering in my room. 'Nath Cottage' seemed to be land of dreams with beautiful Rose garden partially illuminated with cold lunar light. *Our house and that of many others was not ravished as the project of by-pass had found a long pause because of usual problems on government's projects. At times, I wonder whether that was the moment to laugh at mockery they created or the happiness which proceeded.*

Ah…your chattels become so beautifully determined when some of the dreams come true. My feet were not in control, wings were getting added to my sides.

I took the phone out of my coat pocket, while driver was busy parking car under the shade. "I have come. Please come and open the lock."

"Sir, I'm leaving now," my driver said. Before, I could answer him, Trisha appeared in front to unlock the gate. She seemed sleepless, she said, "Dinoo Bhaiya, why don't you stay tonight at our place only?"

"Ma'am, I would have also avoided the tenderness to reach home so late but like how you keep waiting till sir comes in, my wife too remains stirring for me," Dinoo replied. We were speechless for the time.

"Ok, Dinoo. Good night then, you leave. See you tomorrow morning," I dismissed him and moved inside. He soon vanished in the dark riding his age-old bicycle. Again, this action had made me think into yet another issue. According to Dad- *this is the bug which up-brings revolution in the system.*

I slept peacefully that night as I had reached home, almost on the verge of becoming a Member of Parliament as party had witnessed massive victory throughout the Nation with clean majority of more than three fourth of mass. Visionary, they had called me during college days and finally it had begun to happen.

Next day a press conference was scheduled to be held that evening. That was my debut as a Parliamentarian.

❑

18. Politician says, "We are thief."

Sun marked the new day with fast spreading rays. Sunrays are indeed the best example to get inspired from, the discipline and punctuality smells a lot from them. One day failure of them can turn so many complexities within the livelihood of the globe.

I woke up and saluted the rising sun with folded hands, my eye remained closed. I was murmuring, "Give me strength, give me wisdom and courage. I want to spread benefits at a global milieu similarly as you do." It was a kind of oath and a seek stance as well. From many yesteryears, people have been swearing at the name of sun. 'Suryawanshis' are example of commitment fulfiller and disciplined rulers.

Mom came on the terrace to spread the washed clothes for drying. She used to get up very early every morning, and she generally finished up with all morning rituals including worshiping God at an earliest.

"What are you thinking, my son?" She asked.

"Nothing Mom, just envisioning about 'to happen' in the days to come," I replied.

She smiled dotingly, brushed my head by her palm symbolizing the gesture of blessings and said, "Don't think a lot child. You have stepped on that path, which needs lots of courage and only those are even able to step it, who have it within. You are one of them. I have acute conviction in you and in your deeds."

I took mother's palm in my hand, brushed it through my cheek and said, "Mom, I hope that everything will happen the way I want. Though, universe always generally conspires against us."

"No Adi, it is just opposite of what you are saying," she replied patting her hand on my shoulder.

I smiled, and took a leave from there. I had to prepare for the press conference of evening.

Penning of bullets to be discussed about was happening in fire, my pen was reacting at a pace beyond normal. Enthusiasm was high even in a kid of year more than quarter of the century.

Press conference was scheduled to be held somewhere around after the dusk. "See, I just brought it yesterday for you, when you were busy with your Party men in celebrations," Trisha came in floating a new white Prince Coat on the bed. It was a dream dress for me; I searched it many times during marriage ceremony of Akanksha but never got it. It was sold out just few days back, I was in the store. Moreover, this hue was indeed an exotic piece, rare in appearance.

I made a frown with winked smile and said, "Thanks a lot dear. You made my day to follow," and hugged her tight in my embrace.

She tried unblocking my ties and said, "Oh oh…not now, I have to prepare Lunch. Or else Mom will start shouting."

I made a frown, slapped lightly on back of her head and let her go. She broke into a giggle and left.

Day went at a brisk pace; everyone remained tucked to their daily schedule while I stayed busy with one page note.

Soon the immense evening came; I remained seated into the car, which kept ravishing through the forestry road. Streetlights were down, no signs of electron motion within the circuit of passing by residences. Oh, these politicians are good for nothing accept increasing strength of their Swiss saving accounts, forgetting myself being from the same lot. As soon as I reached Matwari Square, I witnessed few young kids by the side, openly enjoying beer and smoking pipe. Unknowingly, 'oops' came from me.

"What happened sir? Is there any problem?" Dinoo tried interacting with me, adjusting the mirror on top.

"Nothing Dinoo! I just feel disheartened watching future of Nation being governed by cheap liquor and smoke," I said removing my spectacles and placing it back to my pocket.

"Sir, it's our slipup itself. We never felt like bolting the right things. If elders would have been in limits and being a white path shower instead of showing the dark path or path of disgrace, scenario would have been much different," Dinoo shared his concern, "Anyway sir, here is your destination."

Many lots of populace were waiting eagerly for me. Reporters had very quickly jumped towards me as soon as I got out of car. They were bombarding many questions to me; many times I felt questions being unanswerable. Soon the proceedings started as I was centered at the dais and surrounded by inquisitive journalists. I don't know how others perceive but to me it looked as if I was the meal of salivating jackals all around. But off the recent times, I had learnt the art of overcoming downing nerves.

"Sir, it really looks to me very astonishing for the way you have kept changing your flavors towards career. Is it following some periodicity?" First sarcastic question came to me.

I smiled, kept numb for the a while and answered, "Mate, you know career is merely an option to achieve the goal. As to me goal is the farthest node, this is actually what you are; the day you breath last. I want to be a person, watching everything arranged in order, means; a complete neat and organized structure. Indeed realizations and learning come with the time, and also one needs to be in system if one wants to do something related to it. There must be only two ways to live, though third one exists as well. They are walking with the decayed system and leaving the things on the fate or in the fingers of Almighty, second one is coming up as revolutionary or a rebel being a change to bring the change. Third option needs you to put your leg in both the boat; unfortunately this can't see a better life. I have opted for the second option."

Questions were being bombarded at great pace and surprisingly initial complexion never shadowed throughout. I was speaking as a fierce fire.

"Generally it is found; politician's election manifesto or agenda doesn't come beyond the paper in which it was scripted. Any comment?" Another journalist asked.

"See, we all have been known for turning down commitments. Even media confirms of presenting truth in front of people, although still you know how truthful they are? The game of

TRP is always forcing some spices from them as well; please don't take any personal confutations. Yes, I admit it is very much watchable for what we politicians do, because media has power to portray, which we don't have upto that extent. Being a writer and a journalist too, I always said, and still say, 'Beware, I will write it down,' so that is the difference. Moreover, on my part I will say, I am here only because I wanted to be a change to bring the change. I am not trying to hit sentiments either by saying, 'I will provide food, shelter, clothes and employment to all,' I say, 'I will try my best to revive the constitution for populace welfare instead of a system friendly constitution, I will try eradicating root cause with root solution. Yes, my concern is to remove poverty, increase employment and reduce crimes but my solution lies to the core. I have planned out the ways by which education reaches to each one of the populace, and please note it, to me education and literacy mean different things. A degree is related with literacy but education is beyond the par of degrees. My focus is like finding the ways by which people don't do crime, instead of screwing people doing crime..." I tried answering the sardonic question at best.

The words spoken by me had potential to draw away sleep of many politicians, if believed the way I spoke. But till then my party men thought me of airing in the same way they used to do.

"There is no answers and proxy to you. What a speaker and tauter you are, you have capability to hypnotize many," said Rajkamal Awasthi and he giggled long, pressing the finished cigarette in the ash tray.

I just threw a petite smile. I kept quiet, as I was fed up of telling lies, but he never noticed the hidden intensions and thought behind my smile. It was a sense of extreme confidence and optimism for him. Night kept mounting with the vanishing liquor in the bottle, we were seated in the circuit house, celebrating and strategizing the way he wanted to. Next day, we were to leave to New Delhi for few formalities and real game to begin. The time I took a leave from him, zero state between night and day had just fallen. Alligators must have made a chime somewhere.

The sayings of Rajkamal from the past so many days, was

clearly hinting me for the personality and thought he had. He was one of the very cheap leaders ever in Indian History. He wanted to earn with so many open fists and at the same time he was one to be easily outdone by wise and intelligent talks to some extent. His credentials, claimed him a Master of Economics from Allahabad University. So, that is an example of bi-product from Indian Education System.

***

That day I could not wake up on time at my own, because of the past day exertion. Moreover, the morning sleep, post to a super tiresome day, is always a big gratification giver. But soon the clinging brass bell sound came to my ear drums, initially it seemed some priest was worshiping in my drams but soon I realized Mom was making her morning rituals done. I spread my arms around, but could notfind either of Kartik or of Trisha on bed. I woke up in a shudder; further Mom was busy bribing god and reading hymns for his praise.

Clock said-only five minutes remaining due for seven in the morning. I had my flight to Delhi that evening. Trisha was preparing Kartik for school; Dad was in his Library making the notes ready for the lecture of the day. My home was truly an example of extreme working class, everyone had some or other and I often felt proud of having such a full of activity family.

***

Aditya's tears start rolling through his eyes. He draws his spectacles down, and wipes through the nose starting at corner of eyes and stopping at just above nostrils.

Narendra comes close to Aditya, and put his hands on Aditya's shoulder, then says, "I have been missing my family ever since long time. It has been seven years when they were killed for political reasons, the so-called brothers, uncles, and aunts never helped there snivel. My return from workplace had left me all alone and dejected. I was thrown out of house and I was left with no other option but with this, what I am doing now." His throat was very clear and without any stammering. The loss of children and wife had turned him into a revenge seeker.

***

Aditya keeps numb for a while and looks into Narendra's eyes, which were burning as fire. The flame of lantern was glittering, in his visionary balls while face was radish and the firm built which he had, along with the wrought iron barrel gun hanging by side depicted him being symbol of revenge seeking violence. But the way he had kept Aditya safe till then, even after knowing his real identity, indeed was a deed of love for humankind.

"Ok, then. We will continue with the talks tomorrow. It's been late, somebody might come to scrutinize. You have your dinner in the meanwhile. Hope now, you must have got acquainted with the food," he says wearing arrest of a smile.

Aditya smiles, and says, "It's fine mate. I don't have any problem eating what you all eat."

Narendra soon disperses into the darkness ahead. Aditya lies on the coconut rope cot. He takes a deep breath and closes his eyes. Suddenly he brushes his whole face by pressing it hard, and gives a solid bang on his head by other hand forming a fist. Again, tears start oozing in his eyes. He rises from the cot, marches in the direction of opening, he peeped outside. Guards were present at a distance of about hundreds of meters, he could not see their face as only black imagery is seen which is in motion within the yellow background of fire.

Aditya gets back to his cot; he opens the cap of the earthen water vessel, puts his hand within and then starts forcing his hand out. After a momentary struggle his mobile comes out in his hand. Very hurriedly, he scrolls down through the folder containing images and opens a picture, which had Kartik and Trisha within. He bends on his knees and brings mobile close to his lips. He bursts into a deep moaning cry, putting one hand on his orifice. Saliva finds way through the gaps between fingers and touches the mud on earth.

Even strongest people melt down after getting touched by the heat of emotions.

He remains lying on the earth, without caring for the surroundings. It was never known if sleep had rolled him over or the fear of segregation was making him high.

Generally morning always brings a new day with new hopes. But, what it had to bring for Aditya?

His eyes open, as someone was forcing him to wake up. Narendra stood up right next to him. Aditya rises up casually, his phone fells down oozing from his lapse. "Oh! I'm sorry…very sorry," Aditya says, trying to recollect it.

Narendra remains numb for few seconds but soon says, "I can understand your condition, but we have to be bound to few things," his eyes turns broad, red plasma lines come visible, "You know, if any one from around knows this, we both will be cut into pieces and will be meal for those wild dogs they keep as pets."

Aditya sucks back dribble, which is resembled by his throat lump's motion. He softly says, "I'm really sorry. This won't be repeated from now."

"That is alright for now. You must be thankful to Almighty, as I have been kept in-charge to take care of you. Sir! It is true; you are a very good man. Your long life is also need of the true *mission of Naxalism*, but at the same time my duties are major as well," says Narendra putting a hand on Aditya's shoulder.

"I am deeply obliged to you mate," says Aditya taking Narendra's hand in his hand.

"Sir, it was your heroic deeds by you as an IAS officer, which made me a distant disciple of yours. You are daring, strong and a visionary man, a rare breed among the recent human species," says Narendra.

"I always knew badly about you people. But now, my perception has changed altogether after meeting you. Now, I also wish to know a little about you and Naxalism operation as well," Aditya says keenly.

"I will tell you sometime sir, when situation really needs it. For now, please tell me what happened after that? You then went to Delhi right?" asks Narendra.

Aditya and Narendra sit on the cot. Aditya again begins narrating the chronicle.

***

Yes, I went to New Delhi after that, to fulfill the official formalities. After I reached there, oath-taking ceremony was organized wherein all MPs blabbered enough of false words. Cabinet of Ministers was formed. I was given HRD Ministry. Gradually, things about Indian Politics were becoming transparent to me. All politicians irrespective of belonging to 'Party in Rule' or 'Party in Opposition' had the only aim of tightening the sack with money and only money. Among themselves, politicians often felt delighted being called the best for be-fooling public.

Indeed thieves are cousin brothers.

The monuments of the Capital city were contributing more to increase content in my patriotism. I habitually used to walk on streets among the crowd, not only this, very frequently my time was being passed by with street shopping. It seemed very irrelevant and waste of time to my party high commands. The situation was so hilarious for them, they needed dozens of gun men while shopping valentine gift for their loved ones or I doubt if they purchased condoms at their own. They said, it was an act of fool, security concerns may arise, but I was never perturbed. My definitions had to bring many troubles for them in future.

I had a firm belief- Leader is like a flop hero of any movie, if he can't sleep, eat, talk, drink and even play the way his countrymen do.

Numerous doubts and interrogating thoughts kept appearing in my brain. I wondered- *Why leaders are so much hyped, they are indeed in the house because public selected them. Why can't they use a bicycle instead of luxury cars for travel? A bicycle would also help them reduce unnecessary fats and also contribute to increase in use eco-friendly measures. As the name suggests- Leader has to lead. A cricket captain will never place himself in a different seat than rest of the players, then why these political leaders? I guess they themselves have increased the chances of crimes against them by creating non-needed adjective of a celebrity. Today there is enormous increase in the sale of automobiles, the biggest contributor of global warming. Had they not used so much of automobiles, public won't have been so fascinated about them either. Ah...it was so simple and petite; they unnecessarily added so many complexities. But who are to be blamed- The Public or the Leader? And what is the solution? Do we need to eradicate these complexities or bring more with added domain of luxury?*

❑

19. Drama at Parliament

The tricolor was swaying in vigorous dynamism. My inspiration since childhood, had taken me aback that day even, hair on hand had turned normal and motion of blood seemed hot with ooze.

I was deeply excited and equally nervous to attend my first parliament session. The dream was in front of me. Some unknown energy were churning my legs in a vigorous motion, as I walked along with Prime Minister of Nation, Virendra Singh, Home Minister, Rajkamal Awasthi and rest of the cabinet. Opposition too was on foot by the side. All honorable Parliamentarians kept chit chatting, cracking dirty jokes for Mother India, I never became their part, and my eye was darted at the entrance door of the hall.

As we reached within the hall, things seemed so monumental and royal in taste. The ambience itself was like–someone will get lured to do something royal but politicians are persons to be felt pity upon, their emotions never erupted.

Not one's lifestyle but one's deeds make one royal.

Dark auburn teak wood furniture looked extremely elegant which rested upon green carpet base. The gigantic Greek ordered column by the side had turned grey and blemished a bit, which spoke of house's experience. The arrangement was like an open thrust stage. I glanced through the interiors like kid of a poor farmer deeply scanning through the building of their proprietor.

It was after long span of time that an individual party had won sufficient votes to form ministry without any amalgamation. We all took the respective seats. In a while, doorkeeper made an announcement for the arrival of the Chairperson. We all stood in his honor and sat down after his instructional nod. The proceedings of house began very soon.

Few members from the Party-in-Rule, started the notching with the explaNation of briefing about their planning in respective ministry. I carefully started listening to the speeches, which were full of many promises and commitments. The words valued almost on the similar lines as that of leaders, I heard of from the past. All appeared a 'Utopia' achiever to me.

Issues remained running at a smooth flow till pre-lunch session. The real drama begun in post-lunch session when, comparative analysis, taking opposition's past reign as reference, started being outspoken. The members of parliament wearing the mask of opposition started attacking the Ministers with substantial debate. Whole Parliament had turned up into a war place.

Right from the day-1, opposition started at variance on rationalization of any notion by the ministry. Very soon the respectability was all lost and nomadic sense had taken upfront. Respected speaker tried his best to uphold the etiquette but whole house was eager to break the breach at max.

How will leaders take up load of regulating whole Nation if they can't regulate their own action?

It didn't take much time when agendas being discussed had started shaping up as delicate concerns. It was painful to see extreme barbaric show being presented by the National leaders. The moment had turned into a fun matter to be enjoyed by me, but on the other edge, I was worried for the hopeless hands taking up responsibility of Nation building.

To my surprise, matter also took up about the formation of cabinet. Opposition had questions upon capability of few Ministers including me and in fact, they delivered extreme fear for HRD being stacked at my hands.

I remained all numb, as nothing much was there in my receptacle to deliver 'for' or 'against'. At times blood started getting frenzied, but never ever, I tried to showcase my guts to them, might be I was bit too scared and nervous to begin.

To my repose and delight, many of the leaders were sacked by honorable Chairperson for the misbehavior and transgression.

It was again a fun watching National figures being fired out of the place. I giggled, but cared not to get it exposed.

The day got over with lots of fireball exchanged, I knew, more were to ensue in the coming days and I had to lead with my views as my desigNation meant for that as well.

Rajkamal informed me to meet him after sometimes at his office, as he wanted to have some important and urgent talks.

***

I went to his office. He was seated on a leather coated timber chair. Office was surmounted with plentiful books and files. I got the feel of him being a big intellect, which later reflected as the real image, which was not more than that of a pseudo intellect.

"Have a seat, Aditya," he instructed me as I entered. In the interim he instructed the peon for refreshments. Initially he started talking with me on a very normal tone, but soon matter's seriousness came projected to me.

"Aditya, this is not the way man. Throng is laughing at us. You are the HRD Minister, but fire seems missing. Were you not being inflamed by the talks and jokes they were cracking at your name?" Rajkamal questioned me.

"Oh…I was truly unable to respond, no answer or justification were burping in my belly at that moment. I was helpless sir," I tried explaining. But matter of the fact was that, I was partially bothered about all what was happening.

Rajkamal giggled and said, "We all know that you have maximum potential, knowledge and fire among many other leaders, but it won't help if it remains known to us only. You have to explode. Man, they were questioning about your desigNation, and that is not less than big slap to whole party."

"I'm really sorry for that sir. Might be first day, came very heavy on me. This won't be ever repeated," I shrugged taking an excuse tone.

Rajkamal kept pouring the tonic of political science in my ear. I unwearyingly kept taking them in, like a subservient pupil.

***

Gradually, I covered up my gaffe. I started being one of the key speakers whom everyone including those from opposition started giving a bound chary hear, as it talked about nobility and incorrupt practice incorporation. Unfortunately the color of my speech was not party specific, defending. My lexis were indeed outstretching about National concern and public welfare. They were honest with no molding, or carving. They were strong and original to nature and certainly it was screenplay of movie, which I had thought to display, though it always seemed usual 'to be spoken' words to them. I never bothered to make their perspective clear at that point of time.

Very often, a tongue twister is conceived to be a magnificent display of oration, irrespective of matter it contains.

❑

20. Leader ≠ Party Man

My undertaking was falling to be on different lines on which party was thinking off. I was indomitable to bring some changes, in the working of system. Trisha and I were discussing about the concern, sitting in the library. She was busy arranging the books, while I was drafting few notes.

"Trisha, this has to be done at any cost. You know these changes can boom away all hurdles for the progress of Nation," I said further scribbling through the notepad.

Trisha was still more concentrated in stacking the books, she replied carelessly, "Hmm…ok."

A frown appeared on my face, I felt dejected and neglected. I stood up banging the notebook on table and moved towards Trisha. I caught hold of her both arms, forcibly turned her around, which made few books fall down and I screamed, "Why are you not listening to me? I'm talking rather imperative."

She made a sour appearance at first, then giggled followed with her attempt to loosen my grip on her and said, "I was listening to you only dear. Why getting so angry?"

She brought her full maw close to that of mine; her warm breath touched my lips, as they were apart with expanse less than an inch. Anonymously, my eyes closed down, and grips loosened on her. I was anticipating bucketing of honey juices in my orifice. But she made a sudden escape giggling to high pitch. I too started laughing and ran after her. After some race through the large library and attached terrace, I finally caught hold of her and she crashed into me. We were breathing heavily; the dark night sparsely illuminated with emaciated moon was very erotic and indeed seductive. That time, our lips met quenching each other's thirst. My body kept playing rhythm through her faultless curves.

Finally after a long lasting cuddle session we got separated. Trisha said, "I have full faith in you. Certainly, success will kiss your feet."

"It's because of my Lucky-Charm. Had you not been in my life it won't have been in the way it is," I added to the talk, "Just let that morning come, when Nation will witness this super change."

"Exactly, but dear what if your party doesn't' support you for it? It might happen, you know all these Educationalists, Coaching Institutes are best pals of the Politicians around, in fact there are many Politicians who themselves do the business of education. And your bill talks about its eradication…isn't?" replied Trisha.

"Trisha dear, I'm a Leader not a Party-Man. A leader is- By the people, for the people and of the people. Here, I'm not playing a cricket match where I have to keep saving wickets and score runs for my team," I explained wearing a smile.

"You are correct from your explaNations, rather you are the only correct but still there is another point, whatever you are doing today is only because, party rewarded you with an election ticket," Trisha argued with me for that moment but her words were indeed falling correct.

"Trisha, actually my loyalty will remain with them if they remain loyal to the people. See, party is in rule because people elected them including me. My being, as a Minister is for two reasons- party rewarding me with election contesting ticket while people electing me as one. Failing of either would have deprived me of getting a place. Party is actually only my reason, but people are both reason and duty," I tried explaining Trisha.

"You know it much better Adi, still I always feel feared for any force rising against you, I witnessed the aloofness when you were busy being a good IAS officer. Even then you were correct to your point but…" she said and further cluttered me into a clinch.

My hands got behind through her back and we were soon in a tight cuddle.

I was fully determined not to remain a Party-Man, leadership was my sole priority. But it was a different ball game altogether for many other leaders. I was busy framing plans to enhance economic, fiscal condition of citizens while for a disparity, mostly all the leaders were busy planning their own fiscal growth policies.

***

"Mate, see the bill you are making will no way attract any lot of Minister. All will run behind you to generate food for their pets. Do you even know this fact that all major Engineering, Architecture, Medical, Management and other professional technical colleges belong to many of the Ministers. And all these are the major finance giver to them; donation is what makes their Swiss Bank account creep higher and higher. And the coaching institutes about whom you are talking indeed take up the buff admission accountability for these colleges," Rajkamal Awasthi said in a high tone. He was trying his best to make me acquainted with the system.

"If that is so, then why not to break neck of all those Ministers and Coaching Institutes, who are enjoying education as a business? No way, selling education can be an option for business, it is ruining our Nation building capability," I showed my concern, by speaking a stretch.

Incorruptibility creates many chances when we might be drawn in a marsh as a cause of halluciNation at the name of muddy puddle.

Rajkamal said, "Aditya, be good to yourself. The system you want to break is like a food web in which we politicians are omnivores and public are plants and animals we need to eat. Now you are a small fish, don't swim in foreign patch to get envy from alligator."

"I cannot help it, sir. This is the way I'm and indeed it is the only motive behind where I stand today," I said filling the wine glass for him.

"Please understand Aditya. You have potential to be a high-quality Politician; I had predicted it right from first address of yours. And this step by you can spoil everything in one say," Rajkamal tried making my thoughts synchronized with that of all counterparts.

"But sir, what about the commitments, which I affirmed in my election manifesto? Won't it be deceitful to the public?" I had put a resilient question to him as I thought, but he had some different set of nerves.

Rajkamal broke into a laugh and said, "That is never in the list of anticipation of public even. They are well familiar with commitment breakers, rather once you start fulfilling what you committed, it will become superficial treat to them."

I looked with still eyes into him; I was shocked to hear such active affirmation of not completing commitments and stating manifesto to be a sham. I replied, "Sir, I see the faith in their eyes. It is next to impossible for me to forget those bashes clearly visible in the nerves through there visionary organ."

"But we have faith in you. What about it? What about party, indeed you are here because of it, isn't?" Rajkamal had put a taunting question up to me.

"I'm very grateful to party for giving me such a great prospect, but sir people too voted me to be in the House," I replied.

"Huh...what do you think? Is it only the vote, which has made you a Cabinet-Minister, there were enough practices from party as well, which made things happen? Don't let me mistrust my own step?" Rajkamal said wearing little agitation.

"Oh...I never knew it and it's really disgraceful and sorry act sir. But whatever it may be, the only fact is that even party should serve and work for National turnover, so that even I do not need to become an anti-party objector," even I replied with lots of sarcastic confrontation.

"Aditya mate, don't get so vexed. Be sagacious and reality believer. Party will uproot you very early if things don't run their way and I'm just trying to warn you against the assaults, which may actually happen if you don't care. Please understand, indeed I'm your well wisher," Rajkamal replied wearing a cupid smile. I knew he was hinting towards some ugly truth.

I just smiled as a reply and left from the place. The concept was transparent enough to me in the form of self-made philosophy because of teaching, which my Father gave–one needs to give up the party cloak if one wishes to jingle system to reach the height of perfection.

Indeed for me, "Party-Man $\neq$ Leader."

It seems bit too different and off track philosophy, party is the medium, which makes one reach to the political venture. But, it becomes very much understood and appreciative if 'we the citizens' realize, it's we who make a party and provide all the laureates they get. Serving people is their duty and any party not doing it with optimum level, must be sacked.

❑

21. Education-System

"So your party was not at all in the doldrums to think about your bill?" Narendra asks adjusting himself on the earth, "But till then only Rajkamal was aware of your thoughts, isn't?"

"Yes, Rajkamal always used to be the first person to know about my initiatives. He had well barbed me about the happenings to come by. But, I never clogged as my intention were white to trueness, and white of politics never overlapped mine whiteness," Aditya explains Narendra.

"But sir, was your bill completely related with the Education-System?" asks Narendra in an interrogative note.

"Yes my bill was all about it, indeed 'Education-System' and 'Professional Sector' came under my jurisdiction," Aditya replies.

Narendra seems getting very excited to hear these lines from Aditya. "Oh my God, I really just can't believe that I'm sharing moments with a National Leader, sir, I'm overwhelmed," Narendra says showing lots of gusto.

Aditya laughs and shares a statement of disdain, "Even I can't believe where I'm right now."

Even Narendra breaks into a giggle and followed with a curious outbrust, "But sir, still my brain wonders for the reason to–why all were taking this education bill so seriously? How was it going to affect to the masses in the system?

Aditya smiles and says, "Earlier I too had perceived for easy implementation of same but gradually realized and came to know that this bill indeed can shot multiple corruption junctures. I will explain you how Education-System is so much related with all happenings in a country, especially in ours."

Aditya begins explaining him about the Education-System

of India and its evils, which can swathe upcoming with the black quilt for sure.

***

India currently holds the most hilarious and threatening Education-System ever.

It was first realized by me when the new pattern of IIT-JEE entrance examination was made some one and a half decade back. The examination pattern was diluted with only lone examination with objective questions instead of two term assesment based on efficient mind twisting questions. The reason presented by HRD Minister of then was that this pattern will reduce mental pressure on students. Then the question arises for the pressure at the institute itself. How will they cope up with that pressure if they won't be screened through the level of examination which compiles the context of studies in campus? Well, it never reduced pressure on students at examination level even, rather it increased the competition, as examination became assessable to many and cut-off score rose up. Neither IITs could be benefited nor the students, only the community to be benefited where those who had sugar coating over bread and butter through IIT-JEE coaching along with associated bureaucrats.

Uproarious seems the situation when someone says that he want to create more opportunities in reputed institutes and universities. You may give them opportunity in a reputed institute or university but who will grant them an employment if they don't meet the minimum requirement as an accredited professional? Even if they somehow get placed in some or other organization (demand generates opportunity) then why should an organization be allowed to play with the National infrastructure building system? It has been a sad fact that the level of all known universities in India has received a heavy setback in recent times.

Well, there is also a saying that, one can never get through the harsh gateways of reputed universities if not coached at any coaching institute. What a punk saying it is indeed? Professional education is all about aptitude not the capability of solving more questions in lesser time at a stipulated place on a scheduled date.

Coaching Institutes can never actually enhance aptitude an

individual holds, but they can at many times help non-aptitude person get through the entrance examination and reach to the concerned college. However that is when all problems begin.

Government then added more number of IITs, NITs and many other reputed brands, saying that it will again give a way to true talent. This was a great step but harassing it turns when a fact comes upfront that even the existing institutes don't have enough professors.

Well, the entrance examination policies of government are nothing but a key to encourage functioning of coaching institutes at wider range. Still Architecture remains the only stream where student is selected on the basis of aptitude rather than brilliance and studiousness on the day of entrance examination. But, then too government wishes to take up new mold of the system, by bringing all professional bodies under one head of AICTE. It kills all probability of the only aptitude test being conducted in the only stream, i.e., Architecture. It has been a sorry state that the regulators have not yet believed that aptitude makes up better professional than super studious muggers.

Not only this, there are many private institutions running in the country as well. Those who are unable to get through these reputed names, try their luck and chance in private colleges. And those private colleges don't leave any opportunity to charge as much donation as they can. Moreover, surprisingly most of the private colleges are owned by big Political leaders. These bequest fees are actually needed for development of college as these colleges are not funded by government but the legal name for that fees is 'Development fees', which is to be charged with a written receipt of having received it. On the contrast, colleges charge it as per the Achilles' heel and non eligibility of a student, weaker is his past academic and entrance examination records more they charge.

Government actually allows fifteen percent seats to be filled under management quota, but there have been instances when colleges make almost three fourth of their seats rated under management quota. And the same authority, which governs the whole technical education never ever found worm sneezing through their ear.

Thanks to almighty, IITs have still maintained the level of

education in their campus, though still they suffer along with the rest of ordinary schools, that is at the par of innovation and creativity. Hardly, we have been receiving any invention or creation from any of these institutes on yearly basis. Luckily or providentially India is the Nation with maximum number of professionals but unluckily and unfortunately least inventions and innovations to its credit. Also, there has been a concern regarding brain drain, both in the terms of stream shifting and country shifting. After graduating from these colleges in a particular stream, people tend to have a change in stream further for post graduation in the name of watching better career opportunities. Young lads often travel to other Nation, once a multiNational company tells for providing a better package than any Indian firm. Though this reason sometimes looks worthy and justified enough, but then the issue must be taken to the Indian firms and companies as well, we need lesser firms with greater quality, not a crowd of nomads, who are just running business at the name of profession. If at all the number of candidates graduating, as qualified professionals, would have been less as per the eminence, these new firms and organizations won't have come pouncing in to provide job opportunity to any up-comer.

Any individual will never wish to get operated by a doctor with null skills, but the same person might dream making his non-efficient son, a doctor or engineer for sure. Things change when it comes to belongingness, so matter will be much proscribed and in limits if people start feeling for realm as own.

So, this was the saga of reputed colleges and deemed universities nevertheless same situation has been widely observed in case of state technical universities, who provide affiliation to many private and government funded institutes of the state. They have been altering syllabus or courses of study as per the viability of faculty in respective colleges. The scene is like that, if faculties of any subject is in scarce, they will simply shut down that subject or rather make it an internally accessed one. Not only this, syllabus is also altered as per student compatibility for confirming maximum students getting the degree. There have been numerous examples, one of the university removed Mathematics as a subject from course outline of Bachelors in Architecture, they also sang the song of teaching Structure conceptually and theoretically rather than with practical numerical examples. Moreover, it was a real shock because, understanding of Mathematics is very essential for knowing about technical subjects of Architecture including the Structures, and the understanding of these practical subjects are very necessary for executing a practical Architectural projects.

Even at the time of evaluation of answer sheets of university semester examination, lots of carelessness is adopted. The answer sheets do fall in the hands of any available person in university, who might have never ever dealt with the same subject.

The colleges and universities have been giving more importance to their university examination rather than practical approach to the situation. Students feel the stress to cover up their examination syllabus prior to understanding of the same. Even if you have written all answers correctly in examination, it never assures you becoming a master of at-least a familiar of same.

Alas! The situation becomes so hostile and hilarious when the reputed companies also give enough weightage to the marks sheet of an individual at the time of placement. A fact is very clear, it is very easy to learn or mug how 'Rome' was created, but indeed more than a challenge to re-create another 'Rome'. When some crisis will arise in a company or even the whole of the infrastructure then it will be the practical credibility of patrons, which will do, not their paper degrees and marks sheets instead.

Moreover, actually indeed all problems of Nation directly or indirectly are related with this Education-System. The reasons why these politicians exploit us or befool us is, only for the matter of fact that we are unable to understand the insight of the laws and constitution which runs us.

The feeble becomes scene when one, who is not at all aware of Agriculture, becomes Agriculture Minister; one who is not aware of Railways comes out becoming Minister of Railways and so on.

It looks amazing to know that if a person was very honest mugging answers and was a feet sucker of teachers, he for surety will come up with awesome grades in marks-sheets with degrees. Moreover, in the quest to find job he is always preferred over any one who was busy doing innovations during the time of examinations, and he ended up with poor grades.

History says best innovators and professionals were either drop-outs or poor at school studies. It happens even today.

***

"Oh, education always meant a source of income to me. That is why, I did a Diploma in Engineering and started functioning as an Overseer," Narendra replies, "in our village my attribute was rated with lots of reverence."

"But what happened at the end, had you been paid properly and had hell lots of money in your possession, they would have never done the same with you. Don't you think so?" Aditya interrogates wearing a wide smile.

"Sir, still I'm not sure how can we replace age old examination system yielding degrees by any new one? Was your bill all about that?"

"Yes. My bill was talking all about that. I had created bill in such a way that it would put clamps on coaching institutes, donation fees, refinement in examination pattern and aptitude becoming job eligibility criteria rather than degree," explains Aditya.

"So, what happened after that talk session with Rajkamal? Did you coin the bill in front of other party members?"

"Yes, I tabled the bill in a party meeting. It was attended by all leaders accept The Prime Minister," says Aditya.

❑

22. New Bill

Everyone was seated in the conference room of the party office. Chit chatting and unnecessary talks kept running through before Rajkamal made an entry into the hall. All of us left our chair and stood up in sense of revere for him, indeed he was Party President and Chairperson of that congregation too. He came up to his seat and made a sit down gesture by waving his right palm. All of us again gained our place on the respective timber chair, clad by white cotton made covers and cushions.

"Virendra *Jee* is not coming today?" asked one of the senior Ministers. Rajkamal replied in a negative nod.

"Well this meeting has been called upon to discuss about party proceedings for the days ahead. Sadly, Virendra Sir has been unable to attend today's meeting owing to health issues. But, he has instructed for the discussions and decisions to be concluded as soon as possible," Rajkamal explains addressing to whole ministry.

All Ministers started exploding with diverse views on diverse points. Nothing seemed relevant, if at all one would have compiled there words, it indeed would have resulted in a book on 'Ways to increase vote bank'. Being in the politics, I was learning numerous *things not to do* as a politician.

"What are your views regarding HRD, Aditya? I mean what homework has been done by you so far?" asked Rajkamal.

"Well, I have thought of completely replacing the existing Education System with a new one, and this is my first agenda of all," I said wearing a smile.

"Huh…we are not in mood of a joke right now Aditya, do you know even what are you saying?" asked an old Politician, "Or else, is there something wrong with you personally, which has made your mental state dejected?"

"Sir, please don't make conjecture without knowing the thing well enough," I reciprocated with an affirm statement.

"So, please explain it to us, that will be better," instructed Rajkamal. My words had given rise to sudden murmur.

"Well, what I'm going to talk about is an education bill, which I drafted many years back, but shaped it finally three-four days back," I briefed the topic, murmur found a pause in shudder.

"Hmm…it seems to be radical and interesting. But hopefully it is not on the lines of Sachin Dev, the ex HRD Minister, who lead his party for a major loss in elections because of wrong HRD implications," the old politician broke into a laugh making the statement.

"I don't care much what he or all other Ministers did and are doing in there reign respectively. It's an output of my personal analysis, which came up being an Architect, Journalist, Professor and an IAS as well," my rationalization proved to be bolt tighter for all around. All of a sudden whole conference room witnessed a pin drop silence.

I started reading out the bill amid the conference.

***

"**Aim and objective**: Smooth flow and implementation of a true Education-System."

"Why do we need such system?"

"It is a well-accepted and known fact that, eradication from root can only be the most appropriate method to deal with any problem. It has been history to present, and soon future will take over, yet problems are same, nothing has changed, even the reason is same, yet we have suffered to find a genuine solution. Let us first focus on those problems, they are:

Poverty/ Unequal fiscal distribution

Unemployment/ Lack in job opportunities

Reservation quota

Non-efficient political leaders

Harassing laws

Lack of education."

However, the matter of the fact is that all these problems have arisen only because of a common root, i.e., lack of a good Education-System. When I say education, it never means the one defined through degrees and gold medals; instead, it is knowledge of some subjects, fields with attribute of humanity.

"Once this system is rectified, corrected or replaced with a new one, all these problems will get vanished at their own. Or rather, I will emphasize on replacement of system because it is suffering through cancer of last stage and it can't be rectified any more. We simply need to replace it with a new one."

"As, I say there is an unequal fiscal distribution. It means either people are very rich or very poor, poor is turning poorer and rich turning richer. This is happening only and only because poor people are deficient of getting educated. The minimal money, which they earn, goes away fulfilling basic needs like food, shelter and cloth. They remain unemployed in large mass, or they keep working in low-grade sectors as labors, masons, peons or even sanitary keepers. Condition never improves as prices of all commodities keep creeping though not really the wages. Had they been educated there would have been employment opportunity in a better sector and hence the condition would have automatically improved. There is again a lame reason lying behind, that is their negligence towards education, they really don't feel like cutting off many things to get educated. Like the first dream, what all these people own, is to get entertained and dressed at best, because this is the lollipop that politicians have been showing to them since ages. Not only this, if the aristocratic class or rich class would have taken pain to teach those working under them, things would have been correct and justified to facts. What is happening here is that destiny is being decided by the birth, deeds are not counting. Moreover, the reason why the cream class is not taking such step is just because, they own the degrees, they are literates in my words, but they are not educated enough to feel like being human and help the downtrodden rise."

"The second problem, I mentioned is unemployment or the lack in job opportunities. This is again happening because of sparse interest of youth in getting educated, if you have scored an ample good marks, this solely cannot ascertain you a job and employment. An individual must be practically sound and perfect with aptitude to get through a job. Also, there is immense increase in number of graduate producing colleges, but opportunities in good sectors have not increased a lot. Job is indeed an output released out of the needs in National infrastructure development, but the raw materials behind infrastructure creation is getting lesser and lesser; hence, lesser work force is needed. We are now shifting towards sustainable and alternative methods of infrastructure building; hence, we need people from different fields with knowledge of alternative systems. In recent times, the crisis has resulted in demand of creativity over credentials, but yet universities don't want to revive their system. Students have been studying same texts, which once his Father had read in the same university."

"There have been many situations when employees have been thrown out, this must have occurred because of their non-efficiency in dealing with the assigned project consequence. Also, there is lack in belief of what student once studied at the university, they don't have enough guts to come up as an entrepreneurs and practice what they studied. This jinx needs to be corrected at an earliest or else our Nation will be ruined for sure."

"The third problem, which I cited, is truly a hot cake for all in the country. It is a matter of great facebook update relevant, a great tweet giver and most happily a great issue for earning a vote bank for all the Politicians. To many points, it seems that it's true, reservation must be given, but rather than on seats, should be in terms of finance. There is actually no way, by which we can play with the National infrastructure building system of country. The moment one lets weaker student become some professional with the cover up of mercy, which indeed will be injustice with the Nation."

"The concept of education loan and financial assessment must be brought up for the economically weaker section. The hilarious situation of education loan system in India says, only those people are eligible for the loan who have enough pay back capacity. What the hell, why will someone seek for a loan if he is capable enough to repay the same amount, why don't better look at the smartness and merit of the student instead?"

"At many times, situation looks pretty messed up, if we consider India of medieval period, then that time lower class was suppressed a lot. They were not let to enter the religious places and shrines; they were devoured of education and knowledge. If higher class started from zero level after independence, then the lower class started with some minus levels. The quest lied in reaching to zero level first and till the time they reached the level 'zero' the rest of Nation had marched far ahead where they couldn't catch them even. Had education prevailed in those higher-class people, they would have tried their best to give lower class people a good boost. But, unfortunately, good talks remained only in the phrases of the text book of moral education. They never came out to be explored and applied."

"Yes, it might deject many of the Politicians, but it's a sad true fact we have been struggling to get Leaders like Lal Bahadur Shashtri and Atal Bihari Vajpayee from ages to say. People are not educated enough to decide for the best Leader, who can sway them on the way to 'Utopia'. Even, Politicians are not educated enough to cater there service well. Please keep this in mind, education means something different to me as mentioned earlier. All the Leaders must understand the importance of good education and apply it within as well for a great prospering Democracy. We need Politicians who are Humanitarian, Socialist and great Educationalists as well. They must know Technology, Agriculture, Science, Literature, Language, History and all which are needed to make a Nation strong. This is a sorry state; in fact, most of the Politicians don't even know our Constitution completely. Moreover, if one doesn't know Constitution well enough, then how will amendments and changes fall in?"

"Laws are an essential parameter for the beautification of an economy or country. However, if we carefully observe these laws deeply, one obvious conclusion will come in then, these laws have been formed carefully safeguarding the authorities and law creators. Let's take small examples in consideration, when an individual's account faces lower balance than minimum required balance or if a cheque bounces back, bank files some charges in form of money deductions immediately but nothing happens to the bank or never they have to pay a penalty if automatically money vanishes from any customer's account for three to four days. When you go to file a complaint, bank officials casually reply- this is a normal case, it happens. You will get back money within next seventy-two hours. What about the loss, which customer would have faced? This is happening because public never realized their own power due to the lack of education within them."

"Lack of education is truly resulting in multiple problems, which are really needed to be taken care of. If once in a while, these problems are solved out, people's entire problem will go away in a fast blow."

"Man, you in every way are pin pointing us," said one of the Politicians.

"Sir, I'm not pinning or pointing at anyone. I'm just fulfilling my duty as HRD Minister of Nation. These are the issues, I observed and framed the bill, which is output of this analysis," I spoke fearlessly. All Ministers sitting around were in a fix. Suddenly, all of them broke into sets of murmurs. Rajkamal kept staring at me, his stare seemed asking me reason for why I was doing so.

I again took the charge and said, "Well, this was the only analysis of the reasons and objective of the bill. I'm yet to discuss it or rather put it open to you all for the final discussion." The conference hall was again set in a silent mode.

"Brother, if your analysis is this deadly and harassing then how taunting and threatening the bill will be as consequence of your analysis. Please, stop being immature and take wise decisions, we all are indeed your well wishers," said another young leader of the party. Worries reflected in his frowning face.

I smiled back and started reading the bill for them.

***

"All the schools ranging from primary to secondary to high must ban private tuitions being given by their Teachers. Preference on marking scale must be given to students abiding this, those getting tutored from outside must suffer for marks. To safeguard financial condition of a Teacher, school will be needed to abide with payments' scheme laid by the Government, failing which affiliation of concerned school will be affected."

"The system of examination at school must be replaced by aptitude tests at various stages, leading to a thoughtful and innovative approach among the students. Promotions of the students will depend on experimental steps taken up by the students, which need to be carefully taken care of by the Teachers."

"Professional stream like sScience (Medical and Non-Medical), Commerce, and Arts must be introduced at an early stage so that student can grow in the field, he is interested in. Even streams like Animation, Design, Architecture and Journalism can be introduced at an early stage to justify a student's aptitude. Subjects can be decided upon after meetings with various Educationalists and experts of concerned field."

"Student's must not be awarded for topping in a class, instead prize should awarded for every innovation he does, might be promotion in class can come up as a result of innovations at faster pace. This will reduce an individual's choice for bribery in life beyond school days. Once, you are doing the things at the greed of getting something in reward, the creativity ends as the job done was indeed done by a slave to a particular gift. When you create by will, you are creative and worth to be praised."

"Entrance examination to a particular field must be made 'aptitude oriented' rather than 'subject absorption orientation'. The earlier decided fields during the school days help with a better screening in a particular field of study. (A student might be a bad scorer in Mathematics in school examination, but might be he would become a great Mathematician to play with numbers and his ideas could in-fruit many new creations)."

"Existence of coaching institutes and private tuitions must be uprooted so that entrance examinations don't rely upon the level of resource provided by the guardian or parent. It becomes an obvious situation that a rich parent will be able to provide his kid with a costly coaching institute and hence he will perform much better than a kid who never learnt tricks and tips to crack a numerical for competitive entrance examination. Rather, let the brains be tested at the entrance level than resource level behind the brain, studies and teachings of Engineering or any other field are to be given once student enters the particular college or university. A coaching institute can only enhance your smartness toward solving a particular problem; they can never replace your brain with a new one. Inventions, discovery and creation don't come only from studies but from an honest study done by an efficient aptitude holding brain."

"All the reputed universities and institutes must increase the cut-off for the students coming from a coaching institute or set different questions for two categories, i.e., Trained and Un-Trained. This will automatically suppress the dirty business, which coaching institutes are doing at the name of education. Indeed what you get from a coaching institute is nothing more than a tonic, whose effect is always due to an end in a while."

"There must be high-end penalty for those charging students against some private tuitions and coaching. Government should organize an aptitude test for all Teachers of Coaching Institutes and those who qualify in the test must be awarded job in various schools and colleges Nationwide. This will not create woe of unemployment for those running the practice of private tuitions and coaching classes. Also, this will strengthen the teacher fraternity of Nation."

"The concept of coaching and extra classes must be introduced by all faculties in all teaching institutions for the weak students (economically, class and academically) free of cost. This can be treated as a duty and must be shifted from teacher to teacher as per the compatibility at institute level."

"Statutory bodies like CoA (Council of Architecture), MCI (Medical Council of India) etc must be formed as many as possible to govern Education-System in a proper manner as per the need of a particular field. Like, right now, AICTE is the body governing many fields, and earlier HRD ministry also tried to place Architecture under the same body, this would have resulted in numerous non-eligible Architects coming up on the show."

"There must be an abolition of admission against management quota at the sake of handsome donation. No Institute, older than ten years, should be allowed to charge donation, the authority must take care that only fifteen percent of the total seat in the Institute is to be filled by management quota, rest all admissions must be done through the well screened process of entrance examination. The colleges existing for less than ten years would be allowed to take donation against some percentage of seats only because they are new and non-government funded institutions. Even, they will have to return three fourth of the total amount charged at the time of student's departure from the college. But college will be free to keep all the interest earned at the capacitating/donation fees."

"Education loan will be provided only to the economic weaker section students at no interest term, where Head of the Institution will be guarantor for the student."

"Studies in college will be based on the research orientation, in which every student will be expected to bring innovation in the concerned field. Instead of university/semester examination, practical assessment system will be introduced for the promotion of student. In this case, a student's creativity, communication skill and in depth involvement will pay back more."

"Even if a student gets a degree, it will never ascertain him finding a placement in any organization. Though whole system will be aptitude based but then too, one with better aptitude irrespective of belongingness to a particular college will be preferred."

"Concept of aptitude test for various jobs will be introduced. Everyone with a minimum schooling will be allowed to appear in it accept few exceptional cases*. A student graduates in Commercial studies, but somehow he finds that he has aptitude to become an Engineer, and then he too may appear in the aptitude test for Engineering. All those who qualify in a particular aptitude test will be called upon for personal interviews and group discussions and then accordingly they will be given allotment in various firms and organizations as per the vacancies available. Allotment will be done by particular statutory body instead of an individual company or firm. For another example, recruitment of teachers will be done by HRD itself through an aptitude test called 'Indian Teaching Services (ITS)'. *Exceptional case: Self trained professionals."

"All the records and academic monitoring will be directly linked with HRD's web portal to enhance maximum transparency."

All heard to me very patiently without making a single fuzz. Many had turned into momentary sleep at the table itself. The reaction was obvious from the in-efficient brigade of dusky Ministers.

***

"It seems you actually don't have any understanding of HRD," said one of the old leaders and he broke into a sudden laugh, "Why did you recommend him mate Rajkamal?"

Rajkamal stared at him for a while, then stared back at me and said, "Are you really sure with your words Aditya? I guess there is some confusion; you need to rethink about it. Isn't?"

"Yes sir, there is some confusion. What I have presented is a summarized draft of the complete bill. I will soon elaborate it to its optimum level and again table it to you able people for final conclusion," I replied with a smile.

"No way, it can be applied Aditya. How is it possible to cut off all coaching institutes and remove the concept of donation? It is indeed following up with income generation for many. How will a private college develop if they don't take donation?" said another Minister from the panel, he banged back his hands on the table as a show of agitation.

"But, there is a provision of providing employment to those based on the coaching institutes. And donation's concept is applicable to the developing colleges, and I know sir, ten years are more than enough to call a college developed. Rest can be easily managed by the fees they charge," I tried explaining the issue to the body of Ministers.

"But then college might hike the tuition fees, again resulting in dissatisfaction among students," Rajkamal added to the ongoing talks.

"Yes, that point is in my mind as well. I need to add a relevant clause for that, so that the fees parameter can be even regulated by the ministry itself," I countered Rajkamal very clearly.

"But somehow your idea seems very vague, rest all can be thought about but mate, that clause relating to donation fees and coaching institutes is not digestible. Let me make it clear friend, I own two big Coaching Institutes, one Medical college and one Engineering college as well. If your rule comes into play, there will be huge business loss to me. Instead why don't you turn a little practical and start sharing something with many like us," said Mr. Subhramaniyam with a cupid smile on his face. The ministry of Railways was under him.

Followed with his confutations, many similar sayings came across soon. The scenario had turned crystal clear to me. The only hope left to me was, Virendra Singh, the Prime Minister of our Nation. I preferred staying silent for the moment post to that.

Numerous talks against the bill started flowing within the conference hall. None accepted but Rajkamal was ready to listen to my points.

It was well understood, major fat is generated only through this cheap business of education, and it always takes lots of pain to lose some fats rather than to gain some.

❑

23. Thieves are brothers

The evening conference had reflected a brutal truth to me. I was certainly trying to fish up with the alligators merely being a freshly born fish in the same river. I was indeed looking for a speedy growth to swallow them all in a once, but unfortunately nature never breaks the rule, people do.

I was lying dejected on the bed. Trisha was still in the kitchen arranging back the things before the siesta. Kartik was sitting on the table, doing his homework.

"Papa, will you please tell me this subtraction? I have forgotten the method of borrow," Kartik called me up.

I was very tired and even in some serious trance but I preferred walking down to him, it had been long when I had shred even a talk with my ardor. I rose up from the bed, and followed up to his table. I sat on the table and said, "Tell me Kartik, what is your problem?" saying this I swayed my palm over his head.

Kartik encircled one of the problems in his book. I looked at it, it was the same problem, which I used to be unable to solve, and my Mom kept banging her head, but I never understood so early. I took his notebook and a pencil and started explaining him the problem. He understood very happily.

"Kartik son, come and sleep. It's been very late, you have school tomorrow morning," suddenly Trisha came and said passing her hands through silky hair of Kartik.

"Yes son, go and sleep now. It's been very late," I complimented the word by Trisha. She added with a taunt, "So finally Papa taught Kartik something."

I made a frown while Kartik jumped on the bed breaking into a laugh. I got out to the lanai; Trisha followed me back after arranging bed suitably for Kartik.

I was looking deep into the stars; few vehicles were still

visible on the Capital's street. Light seemed twinkling all around. Trisha hugged from behind and kissed me on my neck. I put one of my hands running through the bare belly. She took a deep breath and said, "Aditya, what happened in the meeting? It seems that things didn't go by a good way."

I took a deep shrug and said caressing her soft cold skin, "One cannot help good things so easily, because good people are less in this world."

"If world would have had so many good people then, what had been the need for urge for good deeds?" she asked, while her grips kept tightening on me. Trisha had perceived the hidden intentions in my words.

"But, still I don't fear and feel for the consequence to come. I will keep walking in this dirty puddle, might be my clothes can soak away all mud and dirt," I said, optimistically.

"But, I fear Adi, please look little aback. It has been long when we talked collectively anything apart from your political front. Why don't you take care of what is happening to you?" Trisha said, running her fingers through my dense untidily grown beard.

I turned around; her Tops got crushed into my chest. I looked deep into her eyes, as she continued doing the same. I broke into a sudden smile and said, "Dear, how I can be so selfish when my Motherland is suffering at the hands of butcher off-springs of her own, the mean brothers of mine. They are eagerly waiting to cut her down into pieces and serve it to any eater customer they get."

Trisha made a frown, she loosened the grip, she dragged me towards her holding my collar and said, "But you are becoming selfish practically, mine and Kartik's life depends all on you. And indeed it is your responsibility to be answerable and caring to both of us apart from Mother India?"

"Dear you are turning kid," I said removing her hand's grip from my collar and I relieved myself from her clutch.

Tears appeared rolling in her eyes, I could feel some wrong happenings, she said, "Now you feel me getting kid Adi, It's undeniably me who has been caring for Kartik. What have you done since his birth? Do you even know the name of the school he studies in? You are screwing both of us Adi in your revolutionary fumes. This is not correct…not correct at all…" she ran back inside banging the door.

I looked into the sky, disappointed like a loser. None of the star was moving for me, I just pointed my open hands into the sky and made a gesture to beg. But mercy was far behind to fall in my laps.

With every creeping day, probability of bill's implementation was nearing null and simultaneously relation between me and my soul mate was turning tart with a great pace. It is a true fact- I was unable to feel Trisha's tears the way I used to, till a month back from then, to be sure I was badly attracted towards bright morning of tomorrow.

Various furtive meeting between educationalists and political leaders had started, though I was never invited part of the same. The leaders had made it very transparent in the last party conference that my bill meant lots of business loss to many, so there was no way it could be fit into the system. Even my party was not feeling to think about my bill, forget about the opposition.

It was after fifteen days from that conference. I went to Rajkamal to find some probability out of the odd.

"Sir, please wait for some time, I will just inform him about your arrival," said the housekeeper.

I replied in a nod and took a seat on one of those luxurious gigantic leather coated sofas. His house seemed to be shining like a palace with so many costly articles installed all around to enhance the interiors. The teak wood staircase ran internally, which also secluded the space between dining and living. The staircase was shining because of the varnish polish, while a large television was showcased at one of the walls. A news channel was running, which was telecasting some press conference by a leader of opposition. I was shocked to hear, the leader was talking about my discomfort with my own party. He was further talking about my bill, naming it as some bill as a major reason for my chances of leaving the ministry and party both. I blinked my eyes for a while, but the happenings were very true and factual.

"This in fact, had to happen someday, don't be so amazed mate," Rajkamal's voice appeared with a giggle. He had just entered into the drawing room. I never wanted to but my heart dragged me to an opinion that my party was playing ploy against me.

I looked blank at him, with no words to speak.

"The world of politics is not that undemanding Aditya, every way there will be lots of thorns coming in. Now, it is only a comment by one opposition leader, soon rest of the parties will be knowing it as well and might be our own party starts thinking other way towards you," Rajkamal took a seat opposite to me. I was left clueless; the words by him were coming all from the dictionary of unexpected.

"You should have not forget it Aditya, someone who can give you the chair, can snatch it away as well, rest you are matured enough. Isn't?" Rajkamal continued welcoming with nailing words.

I kept numb for some time but soon came back hard on him, "You are very correct. Someone, who can give you the chair, can snatch it away as well. It would take very less time when the chair-giver, public gets into the form."

This turned Rajkamal quite for some time, but soon he broke into laugh and said, "Your smartness is the thing, I would die upon."

"How did this news pass on to the opposition? And what is the final say about the bill?" I asked Rajkamal.

"I really don't know how it went to them. Remember, politicians are politicians, and they are brother when it comes to common safety. Your bill is really going to ravish through the business and economy generation for many lot. Hope you understand my words Aditya," Rajkamal tried explaining to me, "and don't expect anything to happen in regards to bill. Though I never said anything against your bill so far, I personally don't want this bill to go ahead for implementation."

"Sir, this is my first take in the politics, second one definitely will be refinement of our Constitution, which actually all of us feel for. Even now forgetting all the things around, if you think once about my bill by heart, sir, you will be able to do real justice to the issue," saying this I stood up and started walking away towards the exit.

"Wait mate…don't feel dejected, come and have some cold water, cool down, I never wish a ditch for you, rather your success is all in my faith," Rajkamal tried convincing me for the stay but I never cared and took the leave.

One thing was well understood, thieves are indeed brothers.

❑

24. Survival of cheapest

Long back Darwin had given the theory which talked about survival of fittest, but here comes little alteration. Cheapest survives the longest and wealthiest. I was dreaming of a great execution ahead, color of revolution was turning darker and darker. I was ready to keep all chattels on stack while attempting to reach the goal. Again family issues had started bothering me, Trisha yet again had started giving me numerous swears and remembrance of responsibility. Squabbling had become a daily custom, which had started putting an impact on me as well.

"I'm leaving Trisha. I need to meet the Prime Minister, before leaving to Bhubaneswar," I said arranging the briefcase.

"Is it necessary to go now, can't you please make it after Parent-Teacher meet at Kartik's school?" asked Trisha, while powdering the utensils for breakfast.

"No ways. You make it to his school please. My meeting with Prime Minister is very obligatory. I have to try convincing him for the bill, rest none of the party member wish to get it implemented. And if this bill is done, country can become 'Ram's Reign' yet again, or might be even better," I explained Trisha. Those days, hardly synchronization was visible between us; she was busy doing her work at dining table while I kept blabbing without caring. Suddenly, I realized and became numb.

"So, you won't be coming! It's fine, but do you ever realize, Kartik is not solely my kid, he is ours, and apart from being a Leader you are a Father and a Husband as well," she said banging the crockery set on the table.

"Just attending a meeting at school doesn't ascertain a responsible parent. There are many other things around; I have many other responsibilities apart from family," "I shrugged putting a final lock to the bag.

It had never happened before. That day Trisha was compellingly trying to stop me; she ever tried co-operating even when my family's life was on stake during my tenure as an IAS, though, we were having sour time amongst, and I was not living greatest of life. My beard had gone very dense; hair had turned long enough almost resembling a feminine style haircut, altogether complete depiction of a disturbed human being.

I don't know, might be she had got intimation for wrong, which actually happened after that.

***

"Is Prime Minister Sir present inside?" I asked guard.

"Yes sir, he is there inside at the pool, waiting for you," replied the guard.

I went inside, from the side door, which used to lead to his private pool. He was sitting on a cane chair, while a low heighted table was kept in the front. As soon as I reached near him, before he could get a trace of me, his big gigantic pet started barking on me and almost ran to pounce on me. I moved little backwards, and spoke with little lesser intensity than cry, "sir."

"Oh...Bruto, no... no, come here, come here..." Prime Minister rose from chair, got hold of dog by his ear and showed him the direction away from me. Bruto cried a little, before finally getting away from our vision. Moment was hilarious certainly.

"Come Aditya, have a seat. I have been waiting for you since last half an hour," said PM.

"I'm sorry for the delay sir," I said, without producing any excuse and took seat on another cane chair located there.

"Ok, it's alright. So, what will you have in breakfast? It is time for my breakfast," said Virendra Singh.

"You take it sir; I already had it at home. Actually, I wished to share some important issues with you," I replied delivering a lie.

"Oh...you are bit too serious about work than needed. Things keep running and life goes on, time won't return it again. Cherish it to full..." Virendra kept sharing, but he broke his conversation soon as the breakfast had already come to be served, "keep it here and bring a glass of juice for Aditya sir," he instructed the maid.

"That is why sir, I feel like finishing all assignment in, at an earliest. That is the only way to enjoy life for me. Thanks to Architecture, which has made me this way," I said sharing a petite smile.

"This is obvious result of youth, my lad. You will learn with time…first of all groom yourself in a good condition, man. You seem to be very sick with all these large bunch of hair and beard. Even you are not decipherable. Has something gone wrong with you?" Prime Minister showed little concern, which I felt unnecessary for the time being.

I smiled and said, "Thanks a lot for the concern sir. But nothing as such, everything is running so fine and composed. I want to discuss the new bill with you, which I framed few days back. None of the other Ministers are agreeing for what I want to do so I thought of sharing it with you, the most compatible of all among us."

"Ok. Aditya, tell me, what you wanted to share," said the Prime Minister.

"Well sir, I wanted to share my Bill with you. This Bill focuses on refining the Education System," I said.

"Oh yeah, yes, yes. I know it. Rajkamal told me about it," said Virendra Singh.

"Oh, then I need not brief it to you sir." I said.

"Yeah definitely, you need not brief it to me. See actually, it is really very tough to pass such a bill. Dear, you are bit too young and naïve. Practicality doesn't permit us to apply it right now; there are many other issues, which are needed to be thought about prior to your bill. Aditya, remember, your responsibility is bit too big being a Union Minister," replied the Prime Minister.

I could feel the result to come by, disappointment had risen on my nerves, I said, "Sir, this is really discouraging. I'm looking for a bright tomorrow of glooming Nation. It is not so sir, I don't have enough experience under belt or I don't know administration and it is mattering like hell. Prior to being a Parliamentarian, I have spent life being an Architect, Journalist, Professor and IAS as well. And I was approached by your party to get into politics.

If at all, I was naïve, you should have not opted for me and even you should have not given me such a big responsibility called, 'HRD'," I said in a gulp.

"See Aditya, we had taken you in only for the matter of fact that you really are a popular figure for Nation now, and you have full potential to be a big leader. But this attitude may ruin your career in politics," the Prime Minister yet again tried to convince me with fake un-professionally political words. I had well realized his intention by then. My hopes were getting shattered into pieces.

"Sir, if that is the final decision then I don't see my role in this cabinet at all, its better if I resign. And don't worry sir; I won't speak up anything about my resigNation during the address today. I will be only sharing my ideas of the bill, if party cannot decide or look forward for the betterment of Nation, might be then, public can understand and force an application. My departure will be numb one, without much alarm as most politicians," I spoke an open taunting threat to the Prime Minister of Nation.

He stood affixed and stoned for some moment. But soon the Indian political blood sprang its shade, his lips spread wide into a smile as he said, "Why getting so vexed mate. You are like son to me, and I know your capability. We will do something for sure in regards to this bill. You don't worry, you have a great address ahead today, and in the meanwhile I will try affixing best of the solution. As you always say, I will think from grass root level this time." His lips widened even wider for a sarcastic grin.

I replied with a side inclined smile, and said, "Ok sir. Thanks a lot for the support. Trust me sir, I will do my homework at best. I very well remember my oath, which included a line, 'I will be always ready to even die for welfare of my Nation and its people'."

"Wishing you, a good luck Aditya and have a great journey and tackle ahead, we all are proud of you and will ever be," said the Prime Minister as I rose up from chair, taking up the file holding the bill details.

I had well anticipated a dark night to follow me soon. I knew Virendra Singh very well, he was a person of stiff thought and application, and he rarely changed his decision ever.

While leaving, I touched his feet, as a regular custom. And I left with marching and banging my legs fast.

"Oh…Aditya, please keep this copy of Bill here. I will table it in office today evening," said Virendra Singh.

I turned around, kept the file and finally left.

I reached Kolkata taking up a copter; I had my connecting flight to Bhubaneswar from there on a chartered plane post to a meeting with party's regional head. After finishing up with meeting in regional office, suddenly some wrong fishy intentions started pouring in my mind, including Trisha's call of asking me not to go. I cancelled idea of taking a connecting flight.

I instructed my PA to arrange a car trip to Bhubaneswar.

At the time of disaster, our brain stops working or hinting towards wrong path.

It was all dark around, when my journey began in a car. I was sitting at the back seat; my subordinate was stationed to my side while the sole security personal was sitting parallel to the driver. I was soon trapped by a heavy sleep, unknown about the happenings around.

All of sudden my eyes opened, as car had stopped resulting from powerful brakes followed with a similar sound like that of a weeping dog.

"What happened?" I asked, popping my head upfront.

"A long tree trunk just fell down. Thanks to almighty, we all are safe," explained the driver, "Don't worry sir, we will soon clear the road at an earliest."

All three of them got down and started attempting to remove the tree log. The antonym of white was spread all around, not even stars were visible due to overcast environment. Some buzz of insects were blowing all around, at times they were surpassed by resonating sound produced through bamboo as well. I took my left wrist up, but to add to my disappointment, I had missed it. Further, I took mobile out of my pant's side pocket, ah…even the battery had reached null charged. Everyway camel doesn't seemed sitting my way.

I peeped outside from the window, and cried, "What is the time?"

"Sir, it is exactly one 'o clock," my assistant replied. I

couldn't see much of the activities; accept the light beam getting incident from torch in his hands.

*Boom…boom…*gosh, two consecutive blasts came to my ear, followed with sparkling yellow flames close by. Whole car got into its affect and it got dislocated to some extent. *Thang… clang…*front glass came conked out into pieces. Holy shit…it was a bomb blast. Oh, all the employees upfront had got thrown away sprinkled into pieces. I never received any moment to react. I just sprang out of the car, having realized the happening of an attempt to kill me. As I came out of the car, and ran towards the forest, firing started in a trot and again occurred, a big blast. This time it was in the car, it flew up with many sparkling yellow fiery fumes all around. After the fall, it dashed into the forest on other edge of the road. Oh…it was horrifying, trees had begun burning. Huge flames were visible to my eyes, which had widened out of fear. I was able to sense death nearing me, but I decided to save myself. As, I started running away, it seemed someone drilled thick fire rod into my thigh, I stopped for a while and looked there, red jelly had found its way out. Tears took place in the determined, revolutionary eyes. It appeared as I was leaving the globe, that too without sharing the honey words with my honey. Only the faces of Trisha, Kartik, Mom and Dad were appearing to me. The fear to die turned me over optimized with the thought; I started running faster and faster for my life, making my pain irrelevant and partially felt.

They had again played the ploy against me. Almost killed me, but thanks to the 'supreme power', I survived. But, to them matter of the fact still is- 'Cheaper you are, more you survive'.

❑

25. Meeting one from stories

"When my eyes opened, I found myself struck where I'm right now. Rather, I must say, 'I had never anticipated meeting those people, who always remained as an anecdote to me'," Aditya says stretching his arms in air.

Narendra puts his hands in concert for a clap, he rises from the earth where he was sitting and makes a saluting stance and said, "You are certainly a noteworthy being. We have had so many leaders like Netaji, Lal Bahdur Shashtri and Bapu but never in recent so many decades, when our country needs most of them. You need millions and millions of gesture, sir."

Aditya moves forward, embraces him and says, "Don't debase me brother. I'm just doing what we all should do as a citizen. Wherever and whatever I have been doing for long time has one thing in common, i.e. love for Nation and humanity."

"Ok brother. It has been a bit too tardy now. You eat and have a sleep, I'll just bring victuals for you," he says and leaves.

Aditya just shares a petite smirk in a reply.

Few relations emerge so abruptly, unknowingly with those badly perceived people and we end up writing major histories.

Beautiful night with pure circled moon stood upright showering its silvery cold rays, which were falling in squatters forming beams through the pockets in impenetrable forest. From far away, the game between lunar light, tree pockets and tree shadows looked like charcoal rubbed artistic creation, while the orange flames from the vernacular heat where again presenting an artistic edge of mother nature. Far away few black shadows seemed arranging some logs one over another. Overall, the surrounding had a beautiful onset and any person having a creative attribute would have definitely adored it for sure.

Aditya comes inside, and gets seated on the cot. His expressions kept yelling the ravishing beautiful yester memories. Some crazy happenings were lightening the tensed climate inside, at times he laughs, smiles and gets into a sad expression.

"Here it is," Narendra comes in with a plate loaded with many fried, salty and sweet food items. He keeps it by the side to Aditya on his cot.

Aditya breaks into a grin and says, "What happened? Suddenly, atrocious Naxalites have cooked greats for me?" intentional sarcasm is reflected from his saying.

"It's sad, even till now you see us being vicious piece," Narendra says making a frown expression, "though these items have been cooked in bulk tonight, and soon celebrations will begin. Tomorrow is the day of 'Holi-the festival of colors'."

"Oh…yeah, that is what those people are doing there, collecting wooden logs in a pile," Aditya says keeping one of his arms on Narendra's shoulder, "I'm sorry mate if you are hurt. I never intended for so. I was just jesting."

Narendra smiles and says, "It's alright. If you remember well, I had promised to tell you about the aim and perspective of Naxalism."

"Yes, I remember it well. So, when are you going to narrate it for me?" asks Aditya.

"That great day will be tomorrow, when I will be narrating you the tale of an avant-garde attempt. This actually botched in recent times. Everywhere, it's the corruption and greed, which is overtaking the initial goal and aim, may be politics, administration, education, etc. it prevails everywhere," explains Narendra, "Ok, then you can have a sleep for now, after having eaten these eateries."

"Come mate, we will eat together," Aditya offers Narendra to dine with him.

"No…no…you carry on. I have some other thing for me to dine. I need lots of pain killers," saying this he pounces towards a molded shelf at extreme corner. He clutches one of the black bottles out of three and keeps it near to the eateries plate and asks, "Will you also like to have it. Trust me; it kills hell best of the pains. You might feel better."

"It's fine, Narendra. I don't have loads of pain as you have, and rather you should trust my ways, might be something can replace these colored liquors, I cantilevered myself once freely trusting it but all came as no aid," Aditya says wearing a smile, "by the way, Narendra…we are talking so freely over here. Isn't any one at surveillance on us?" Aditya shows a concerning vision.

Narendra soon seeks an alarming pose, he draws he barreled gun out and points at Aditya and says, "Hands up..."

Aditya raises his hands portraying a sign of aghast; he appeared extremely shocked by sudden change in behavior of Narendra, as his eyes turns larger and lumps starts pulsating.

Very next two armed men come into the space. "Narendra, what happened? Was this bastard trying to escape?" asks one of them staring deep at Aditya.

"Hmm…not exactly, you all don't fret. Trust my worth, I'll manage him well," Narendra replies, further coming closer to Aditya.

Other individual comes even closer to Aditya, he points his finger towards him and says, "Never ever do it again."

Lots of terror becomes clearly visible in the eyes of Aditya, and for the matter of fact it was taunting him even more as it was out of a shudder. Soon the two persons depart away. In a very next set of action, Narendra moves and runs towards the entrance of the door from inside. Now Aditya's face seemed blank without any expression, the words and speech, all had dried away in a while.

Narendra again comes close to him, throws his gun away, and bends his head facing earth so that his long hair had made a curtain between him and Aditya.

"Ha ha ha…" Narendra raises his face and accompanies a long laugh, then says, "You were amazing; your nerves seemed to have dried out of blood. You were all white and pale…sir, the world is even more acerbic. You say that you want to revive this system. Which is not at all possible, if you fear, the way you did few moments ago."

"Oh…you played a prank on me!" asks Aditya in a low tone. But soon spreads his lips wide in a smile followed with a pat at back of his cranium.

"No sir, I was doing my duty in reality. That was what,

I'm actually expected to do. Isn't?" replies Narendra with an intelligent smile.

At times breaking the rules and breaching the duty protocol is the need for broadening of mankind globally.

Aditya smiles and scratches his dense untidy tousled hair. "Yes, I understand," Aditya says, and sits down picking up one of the fries from the plate, "Join me Narendra, with whatever you wish to."

"Yeah, sure," he sits besides Aditya and opens up his bottle of liquor. In the meantime, noise of Holi celebration had begun outside.

Soon after having done with dinner, both of them lay down for a sleep. Narendra soon dozes off because he was very high till then, while sleep seemed miles away from Aditya.

Remembrance of past Holi at home starts knocking at his brain. From childhood to the college days, with Commissioner's office to Trisha's home…one thing was always common in all- he used to try his best to escape away as color remained fear for him.

Mosquitoes' feast seemed yet another obstacle between him and sleep. Finally, after a long struggle with agony of past and environment, catnap falls in his eyes. He sleeps there carefree about the happenings ahead. A smile continuously stayed on his face remarking the sign of focusing homely fantasies.

Next morning was full of colors and celebration across the Nation. Even the habitat of Naxalites was getting dyed and yells of "*Holi Hai…*" was enchanting the climate all around. The partially cold morning waft too justified the incoming new season. Aditya wakes up hearing the celebratory noise all around. All of a sudden, he makes a frown, his fingers pass on to his partially visible lips through the bushy moustache. Lips seemed having received few cracks and touch of fingers resulted in blood getting tucked to it.

Color of nature can never be avoided.

Soon Narendra enters into the hut with powdered red color in his hands. He says, "*Happy Holi* brother, may lord *Krishna* make you reach on the top of success," and covered Aditya's forehead with color. Narendra was blue, red and green from top to bottom. For the first time, he appeared not wearing uniform… he was in *Holi* celebration dress code.

"Same to you too Narendra, you know…" Aditya takes a pause and doesn't continue.

"Yeah, tell me, what you want to say," Narendra asks him to complete the sentence.

Aditya's eyes, turn moistened with the liquid of emotions, he says, "Leave it man…just the family. I sense missing them." And he busted in a deep howl. Narendra tries to console him.

"Taste of victory is only known to the player who struggles at the ground, not to the spectator supporting and cheering for him. You have to pay something indeed, if you wish to watch that morning you have been waiting for seeing as long," Narendra tries explaining, he further says, "But I don't have my family alive yet, so that I can even…"

"I can understand mate. You really took up all pain very strongly, but at many occasions, I wonder, a person like you working for a militant organization. Why is it so?" Aditya further puts a toe crushing question. He comes forward and keeps one of his palms on one of his shoulders.

"You don't know it well then Aditya sir," replies Narendra.

❑

26. Villain is real hero

Naredra closes the entrance door and asks Aditya to take a seat. They both seated together while the hooligans keep enjoying the moment with Holi yell and songs. He also instructed the guards to stay outside. Today, he didn't carry barrel gun with him but soon he takes out a revolver from the side pocket of the kurta he wore and places it on top of the earthen pot's cover. Aditya looks astonished and his eyes get stuck to the revolver.

"The things that will happen today can turn your life around Aditya sir. Moreover, even the chronicle, which I'm narrating can add flavor for the same," says Narendra.

Aditya keeps frozen for some time, he gulps some saliva, which seemed stuck for a while and says, "Ok, so what is that?"

"Well first you need to know some stories," replies Narendra.

"Oh…wow. I'm all ears, please narrate the saga soon," Aditya urges.

***

Narendra starts narrating the tale, "I belong to a small place called Bishnugarh, rather you can say, 'I belonged,' located at a distance of around an hour drive from your hometown. I was married just a year back from that incidence, and was staying there in a joint family. Often, I had to be on site visits owing to my job as an overseer in the state electricity department. Everything was running so well and organized. I earned less but my aspirations were limited as well. The only problem, which my family and I had to face was trouble at the hands of relatives and cousins. I was the youngest and was hardly able to contribute a lot to family as others had been doing. Just a single chance and they would have thrown us out of the house."

"Oh…means, you were deliberately under pressure," says Aditya shrugging.

"Yes, actually…that was the case, but life till then was not showing much hurdles on the way. Suddenly, it started happening.

Our village was not being supplied with enough electricity, there was hardly an hour of current for a week, and it continued for a couple of months and was still on. I was sent to local head office since past one month. Villagers had started picking up agitation against the department. Many had a say, 'This bloody Narendra is a useless chap. He can't even assure electricity in his own village? We have been supporting him monetarily, something must be broken.'…another pressure was in form of loan, which I was not capable to return…Saturn finally decided scripting my destiny. People came up in agitation; they set my house on fire. It was the mammoth size of joint family, which helped to flush off fire. But fire had started burning with full force against me. My brothers and relatives claimed me as reason of the fire at house. In my absence they dragged my wife and three month old son out of the house on street, they pleaded a lot in front of them, but nothing crawled in their ears."

"Oh mate…a life full of agony and irony," Aditya says, puffing his hands through the long hair, "I can already feel my eyes moistening with the sorrow song of yours."

Narendra takes a deep breath and says, "What I'm narrating you now, may break you down. But indeed this is a brutal reality. Yes, it happened! My wife was not given place anywhere, not even at her mother's house. They had objection to accept a woman dejected from her husband's house…Ah…" Narendra breaks into cry, he digs his face into the thigh, and he tries snatching all his hair. His buried sounds of weeping were clearly audible in super silent environment inside.

Aditya comes closer, takes a seat in front of Narendra, resting all load on right knee while he places one of his hands at the thigh, which sprawls out due to the bent knee. He says, "It's true mate, no other can actually feel in real the pain one has gone through. But being a human, I can definitely sense what pain of losing someone own means. Hats off to you, that you bounced back so well…but it is till not clear, that how actually you landed up being one among the group of militants. You had a government job at hand. Government must have contributed best to help you out."

"Aditya sir, what are you talking? Is government ever been for the people? This chattel or attribute only finds a place in our Constitution. It has nothing to do with reality," Narendra starts narrating rest of the story, "In order to feed on, my wife started looking for some job and work. Everyone disagreed to support her in worst of the times. I remained unknown, as due to lack of money, I was unable to purchase a new phone, as old one was tapered due to some heavy site works. I remained unknown and mishaps kept approaching…after many days…" Narendra again gets numb and silent, but continues, "Dead body of my wife was found in the nearby river, and postmortem report certified a rape prior to murder. I could never find my kid."

Narendra kept loosing tears all the time along. His nose had turned cherish in shade while eyes seemed getting in the blood tinge, with swollen overlay.

"When I came back from the site work, even I was thrown out of the house. I tried my level best to establish myself back, taking reimbursement from the government, but they never felt like sharing my pain. My agitation against government and my own people kept mounting. Shocked in the terrible pain and losing shade, I sat whole night drinking, drinking and drinking with my oldest pal of time. He was a cobbler by profession. The halluciNation and highness post to drink made me converse with him, which scripted my final destination. 'Yes, mate, these Naxalites really help poor and sufferers. They have been campaigning and firing against government and bureaucracy since past half century,' said my pal. 'That is fine, but will they help me? I'm lost all the way; no ray of hope seems coming in,' I asked him. 'Yes, they will help you for sure and give you an employment also. I'm disclosing you a secret, whole day I work as a cobbler, but at night I'm their employee and that is how I'm able to earn atleast by which some day I will get my daughter married,' saying this my pal gave me some names and address. I never delayed, just the next sprawling day, I rushed to the place and I became what you see me today…that's all mate. This is the chronicle of a loser. My childhood must have never envisioned me this way…hah… though this is a fact. Ah…the unpredictable life," Narendra finally puts a sign of full stop by a glittering smile.

It's not people who are wrong, situation and environment crafts them that way.

"I'm feeling very depressed after getting an ear to that suffering…indeed this bloody life…" says Aditya.

"Well, sir, I'll like to make it very clear to you that actually these Naxalites or the Maoists are not that bad as they have been perceived or portrayed. Not at least their goals and objectives," Narendra makes a new point.

"Please explain it to me that will be better. I have been anxious to know the hidden reality," Aditya makes an urge.

***

Narendra starts narrating all about Naxalite movement, "This is the generalized word used to refer the militant Communist groups operating in various parts of Nation under different organizational envelopes. In our eastern parts, they are referred as Maoists. It is said that they are being lead from China. They have been declared terrorist organization under the 'Unlawful Activities (Prevention) Act of India (1967)'. The term 'Naxal' derives from the name of the village Naxalbari in the state of West Bengal, where the movement had its origin. We, 'Naxals' are considered 'far-left radical communists', supportive of Maoist political sentiment and ideology. A section of the Communist Party of India (Marxist) (CPM) led by Charu Majumdar, Kanu Sanyal, Ram Prabhav Singh and Jangal Santhal, J P Inspector initiated a violent uprising in 1967. On May 18, 1967, the Siliguri Kishan Sabha, of which Jangal was the president, declared their readiness to adopt armed struggle to redistribute land to the landless. The following week, a sharecropper near Naxalbari village was attacked by the landlord's men over a land dispute. On May 24, when a police team arrived to arrest the peasant leaders, it was ambushed by a group of tribal led by Jangal Santhal, and a police inspector was killed in a hail of arrows. This event encouraged many Santhal tribes and other poor people to join the movement and to start attacking local landlords. These conflicts go back to the failure of implementing the 5th & 9th Schedules of the Constitution of India. In theory, these Schedules provide for a limited form of tribal autonomy with regard to exploiting natural resources on their lands, e.g. 'Pharmaceutical & Mining' and 'Land Ceiling Laws', limiting the land to be possessed by landlords and distribution of excess land to landless farmers & laborers. The caste system is another important social aspect of these conflicts. Mao Zedong provided ideological leadership for the Naxalbari movement, advocating that Indian peasants and lower class tribes overthrow the government and upper classes by force. A large number of urban elites were also attracted to the ideology, which spread through Majumdar's writings, particularly the 'Historic Eight Documents', which formed the basis of Naxalite ideology. In 1967, Naxalites organized an All India CoordiNation Committee of Communist Revolutionaries (AICCCR), and later broke away from CPM. Violent uprisings were organized in several parts of the country. In 1969, the AICCCR gave birth to the Communist Party of India (Marxist-Leninist) (CPI (ML)). Practically, all Naxalite groups traced their origin to the CPI (ML). A separate offshoot from the beginning was the Maoist Communist Centre, which evolved out of the Dakshin Desh group. The MCC later fused with the People's War Group to form the Communist Party of India (Maoist). A third offshoot was that of the Andhra Revolutionary Communists, mainly represented by the UCCRI (ML), following the mass line legacy of T. Nagi Reddy, which broke with the AICCCR at an early stage.

In 1970, the Naxalites gained a strong presence among the radical sections of the student movement in Calcutta. Students left school to join the Naxalites. Majumdar, to entice more students into his organization, declared that revolutionary warfare was to take place not only in the rural areas as before, but everywhere and spontaneously. Thus, Majumdar declared an 'annihilation line', a dictum that Naxalites should assassinate individual 'class enemies' (such as landlords, businessmen, university teachers, police officers, politicians of the right and left) and others. Throughout Calcutta, schools were shut down. Naxalites took over Jadavpur University and used the machine shop facilities to make pipe guns to attack the police. Presidency College, Kolkata became their headquarters. The Naxalites found supporters among some of the educated elite, and Delhi's prestigious St. Stephen's College, alma mater of many contemporary Indian leaders and thinkers, became a hot bed of Naxalite activities. The Chief Minister, Siddhartha Shankar Ray of the Congress Party, instituted strong counter-measures against the Naxalites. The West Bengal police fought back to stop the Naxalites. Somen Mitra's house(a Congress MLA from Sealdah), was allegedly turned into a torture chamber where Naxal students from Presidency College and CU, were incarcerated illegally by police and the Congress cadres. CPI-M cadres were also involved in the 'state terror'. After suffering losses and facing the public rejection of Majumdar's 'annihilation line', the Naxalites alleged human rights violations by the West Bengal police, who responded that the state was effectively fighting a civil war and that democratic pleasantries had no place in a war, especially when the opponent did not fight within the norms of democracy and civility. Large sections of the Naxal movement began to question Majumdar's leadership. In 1971, the CPI (ML) was splitted, as Satyanarayan Singh revolted against Majumdar's leadership. In 1972, Majumdar was arrested by the police, but he died in Alipore Jail. His death accelerated the fragmentation of the movement."

"If it was a movement with so much vivid energy and force and even if the cause was noble. Then why did it fail?" asks Aditya.

"I won't say it has completely failed to achieve all goals. It appears a failure organization only and only because it took the root of militancy, extremism against government and the image is indeed created by leaders, administrators and bureaucrats. By the way, now I will tell about few reasons behind movement's failure."

***

Narendra starts telling the reasons behind failure of movement, "In a methodical study, Sailen Debnath has well surmised the consequences and reasons of failures of the Naxalite movement organized by Kanu Sanyal and Charu Majumdar. He writes–The Naxalite movement though continued intensively from 1967 to the middle of the 1970s and resurfaced after some years, could not go a long way achieving anything commendable because of the following reasons:

The Naxalites wanted to enfold the towns and cities by the villages, i.e., they wanted to encircle the urban centers with organized peasant forces of the villages. If the peasant militia could have occupied the cities, according to Majumdar, the so-called bourgeois, government would fall making the passage to the coming of a socialist government; but the Naxalites could not and did not come up to a stage capable of organizing the peasants and thereby encircling the towns.

Majumdar gave sole importance to secret organization, and justified the policy of continuing the Movement without the need to build any popular mass base, forgetting or ignoring the fact, popular mass base is the basic criteria of any Communist-Leftist Revolutionary movement. Kanu Sanyal, the original founder of the movement vehemently did oppose this wrong action plan, while being interred in the 'Parvatipuram Conspiracy Case'. Armed training for the purpose of eliminating 'Class Enemies' was preached, but educating the cadres on the Marxist-Leninist thought process was never taken up, resulting in a lions majority of the cadres coming out of an urban-frustrated-middle class background without any Revolutionary teaching and zeal, and who were desperate for senseless actions. As the Naxalites did not have mass level organization, they lacked mass support. With only a few armed elements, and those not properly educated in the party line, little could be accomplished.

'Khatam' (the action of eliminating the so-called enemies in villages) was a wrongheaded attempt for political mobilization, which was based on the murder of selected people, whose political class and character was never adjudged by their socio-economic conditions or the properties they possessed but very often only by their political affiliation or by the name and color of the party or parties, they directly or indirectly belonged to. For example, in Jalpaiguri and Alipurduar, they killed some petty jotdars, who otherwise could have been comrades in action against the capitalists or could be friends in a revolution for radical change. Moreover, which blatantly shows the 'Myopic' lack of vision of the so called leadership and the party workers.

Recruitment in the Naxalite party took place in the absence

of proper judgment and scrutiny of the political characters and behaviors of the recruits. It was not uncommon for recruits into the Naxalite party to vent their personal animosities by identifying their personal enemies as class enemies, to be killed with the help of the Naxalite organization. Even murders and homicides were carried out by anti-social and hoodlum elements directly under the patronage and protection of the ruling Congress (I) and the main opposition the CPI (M) party, to discredit the Movement.

The ruling Congress party inserted spies inside the unguarded Naxalite organization to gather information about its secret bases and arrest its supporters. Government intelligence personnel and police disguised as Naxalite sympathizers/supporters could easily infiltrate the party's inner organization and arrested many of its leaders, including Charu Majumdar. Thus, police had information about the movements of Majumdar after he had gone underground in 1970, and he was arrested in Calcutta in July 1972. He died in jail days after his arrest, probably in the night of 27th or 28 July. It is not clear how he died, although the government reported that he died of a heart attack. After the arrest and detention of the original founders of the movement–Kanu Sanyal and Jangal Santhal, who were based amongst the peasant-farmers and the tribal laborers of the tea gardens of rural North Bengal, when the leadership passed into the hands of people, majority of whom belonged to the urban-educated-opportunist-middle class, as an 'agrarian-rural-peasant-laborer-communist revolutionary' movement, Naxalbari Movement had lost its genuine character and nature, thus coming to an 'incomplete' end."

***

"Oh, so…this has been the legend behind. It had really a wise objective, though still I believe the path was not correct," insists Aditya.

"Dear Sir, it is really very tough to understand the underlying fact…when rage opens up all bolts, sufferings become a routine, then weapon is the only way to get your rights back," Narendra further emphasizes. He bends down, removes the lid of earthen pot and drags a glass of water out. He gulps all of them in a stretch.

Narendra further adds, "Sir, you are correct. The path of ours is not correct. You have taken the right path and your presence in our society is damn necessary for betterment and welfare. I have an idea, it will help the beautiful dream prosper more and more."

Aditya smiles and says, "So, what is your plan? I'm too dying to get the great bill executed and hence bring in the needed change initiator in the Nation."

Narendra instructs Aditya to come closer to him and take a seat together at the corner on the earth. Narendra takes out a thick, big bundle formed out of black cloth wrapped around. He hands it over to Aditya and says, "Sir, this is an amount of rupees three lakhs, the share of my earning as a militant so far," he further handover the mobile SIM card and wallet to Aditya, "Take these all, sir. The mission has to be accomplished at any cost."

Tears comes ornamenting the eyes of Aditya, he takes Narendra in a tight hug. Aditya couldn't come up with any word.

"Sir, never ever think that this is a good will. I'm not helping you, I'm helping my Nation. Go away sir…go away…Nation needs you," Narendra says.

Aditya wears a smile on his face, a sign of momentary triumph appears, and he says, "Yes, Narendra…yes…"

Narendra becomes serious and focused in expression, he instructs Aditya to leave the place as soon as possible, he says, "Leave quickly, whole gang is high, post to the Holi celebration, drink has played the card for a good cause. Take straight through the visible patch of path…you will be on the highway soon. And take this revolver for safety in case of worst emergency."

Aditya leaves the place; he had received an unanticipated rescue. But no second thought came through his mind for what happened next. Narendra had betrayed his gang and sentence was necessary.

Only five minutes had past from Aditya's escape. Narendra opens up the shelf located at corner of the hut. He drags out a cotton bag; it contained few sketches portraying his beloveds. A diary also came out, which contained various poems he scripted in as a memory output. He wears a prominent smile before finally setting whole bag on fire.

Finally, Narendra had lost it all; he was bursting into a weep. Tears were rolling down like vigorously flowing river; the strong red rebel was on his knee. His both hands stretched facing upwards as his face too faced sky; one of his hands contained the life quenching revolver. He murmurs with weeping roar, “Forgive me…forgive me…I have to do it. If I fell weak now, then I may turn weak again ahead, which can break the noble thought of noble man…Hey Ram!”

Rit…rit…thin line of blood had found its way from the temple. Narendra was gone.

Narendra had sacrificed his life, because he never wanted the story of Aditya known to others from the gang. Indeed, he spent whole of the life as a hero, being a Maoist he was not a villain.

❑

27. Chanakya Neeti

Aditya reaches capital city of Bihar. The spaces in the city were very much recognizable to him; he had spent quite few months and then a year during summer vacation post to matriculation and during his tenure of IAS respectively. Aditya never cared to cut off his long hair, beard and moustache as it was flushing off all probability for him to be recognized. Aditya yet again appears as 'Adiraj Shrivastava, a primary school teacher'.

"Yes sir, electricity, water, everything is properly available in this place. You won't face any problem staying here. Though space is minimal, yet very organized with sufficient light and ventilation," explained the house owner lady while showing the room to Aditya. It was a first floor bargain with a single room, attached washroom and separate stairway. Two large windows were located on two adjacent walls, as one of them had a clear view to the main road in front of the house. The walls were dull white in appearance, lime paint seemed leaving wall at places, but this was more than enough for Aditya.

"Sister, this place is good enough. I have liked it a lot, so can I occupy this place right now?" Aditya asks the lady puffing few patches on the wall, "I'll pay you the advance security deposit this evening itself."

Lady soon wears a wide smile and says, "Yes, sure. That will be so great. Ok, then you keep arranging. See you again in the evening."

Aditya greets back with a smile. He starts setting the bargain for his livelihood.

But Aditya had not forgotten the real mission. The bill was on his mind.

Midnight was approaching. Aditya peeped through the

window, nothing seemed visible except few dogs and bats flanking by the side of building. He takes out one of the four blank ivory sheets; he pastes them on one of the four walls. He ties his hair into a knot, picks up a thick marker pen, black in color.

Aditya was totally unplanned of the exact actions. After long-long years, he was drafting a plan using a marker, though it was not for a building or space. It was for the execution of a bill relevant to the National benefit, rather we can say, he was trying to reshape India.

He starts scribbling so many flow charts and illustrations; it was not an easy job. Indeed, he had to look for a plan, which doesn't fail or holds least probability to fail.

He finally scribbles following bullets and sees them as a vital target:

Media has to be the driver. I need to cover up maximum aspects of media, like print media and electronic media.

Print media will range from journals to daily newspapers, while electronic media will range from television news channels, radio telecasts and internet news sources.

Social networking as well can help to promote the cause.

He was decided with the assault deeds. He was supposed to get his bills published in tits and bits through these media sources. Media always promotes anything, which enhances its TRP. This bill must be a big cover-up, which has remained hidden due to the dramatized death show of Aditya.

Aditya was about to tell a truth, though path was a black one. Chanakya had once remarked, "Good needs to be enforced at every precious cost, irrespective of the method by which it comes through."

Soon he does up with the methodology to be applied. He started thinking about it deeper and deeper, as he lied on the bed, with open eyes directed towards the ceiling, watching the rotating fan blades. His hand remains stationed on forehead, demarcating a thought process going on, while his other hand brushes bushy dense beard. Thinking normally puts a tar on every human brain; Aditya's eyes start jingling slowly and start turning reddish. Sleep starts taking over him...two hours had already passed by after the midnight.

Aditya had already made a lots of decisions last night, though the arrangements of tools for execution was still due.

***

Morning glooming rays alarmed Aditya with its heat. He wakes up in a shudder, the environment inside almost matched with that of outside for the matter of fact that he had not put any curtain and March heat was pouncing in with full flow.

Aditya gets into the washroom to get freshened up. He looks anxiously at each parts of the small room. He soon starts arranging the things in the room placing them to best and efficiently.

After having arranged the room he takes out the total sum of money, which Narendra had given to him, he segregates some amount out of it and puts it in the inner pocket of *kurta* he wore.

He comes out after putting a small lock at the door. He looks all around once getting on to the street. It seemed to be a busy surrounding. His eyes start searching for some snacks with tea, a small tea stall appeared at the corner of the road. A man stood behind, he was busy jingling tea within containers. Also, few plastic lid transparent boxes seemed placed in the front. Those boxes contained varieties of biscuit and toasts. The man was short; he wore a circular Islamic cap and a white vest, which was immaculate with countable russet dots of tea. Aditya smiles a bit and makes a hand waving signage to the storekeeper, querying if tea is available. The man smiles and waves back to call him. Aditya smiles and moves ahead toward the stall.

"Brother please give me a cup of tea," Aditya asks the man.

"Yes sir. Just giving, please have a seat, it will hardly take maximum five minutes," man replies pointing towards the bench kept in front of the shop. Man wore a tied *lungi* and a locket with regard to some religious view hung to his neck. He looked to be an Islam follower by the appearance he had.

"Yes brother, in the meantime I'm taking few biscuits," Aditya says dragging biscuit out of the lid box, "By what time do you start your shop?"

"Yes sir, definitely. Oh, my small tea stall begins generally at seven in the morning. Today, I got a bit late because of some family issues," replies the man.

Aditya starts chatting and sharing views with the man. "I

have just shifted in that nearby lane as a paying guest, it has been just a day," explains Aditya.

"Ok sir, is it in the house of Colonel Manjeet?" asks the man, "What do you do sir?"

"Yes…yes in the same house. So it seems you know that family," replies Aditya, "by the way, I'm a school teacher by profession, I have just shifted here for some research work, which may last for a maximum of six months." Aditya had become a master situational phony by then. His perceptions were clear, a lie spoken for a noble cause ahead is indeed much better than the truth standing as an obstacle for the betterment.

"Oh that is so nice sir. It's really a pleasure meeting a teacher. Sir, I have a request, as you are teacher and off from your job for few days, will you please help my kids do something good in examination?" Man keeps talking with Aditya, least caring for so many other customers hanging there for the tea.

"Ramdin, is tea ready?" asks one of those quid customers.

"Ah…being regular chaps too, you all can't show little patience?" Ramdin says filtering tea into the container.

Aditya smiles for the situation. He asks a boy sitting adjacent to him, "Where can I get good computer or related accessories nearby?"

Boy looks at him wearing little aghast, his stare covers Aditya top to bottom and then he tells, "you need to reach S.P.Verma road for that, it is some couple and a half kilometers from here."

"He is a teacher, his name is…oh…sir what is your name by the way?" asks Ramdin converging the conversation between boy and Aditya.

Aditya again smiles, and says, "Adiraj Shrivastava," he forwards his hand for a sake hand, "well, hope I will get any brand of laptop there in that shop along with internet connection accessories."

The boy turns further confused, he replies shaking hand with Aditya, "Yes sir, for sure."

"Sir, please take your cup of tea," Ramdin replies forwarding the cup of tea to Aditya.

"Oh…thank you…thanks. How many bucks?" asks Aditya as he sips first sip, making a slurping voice.

"Let it be sir…you are a teacher, and being new at my shop, guest too. Let it be a gesture from my end," Ramdin says adjusting the towel on his shoulder, wearing a petite smile, "Please take care of my request, sir. Do teach my kids, they need some really good teacher, they have been crying from many days to get a coaching institute but I'm a poor tea seller sir, how can I afford it?"

"Oh…how much these institutes usually charge?" asks Aditya.

"I don't know the details sir, but it's known fact that these are extra flavor, which is never actually needed. I have a belief, food should be simple and nutritious enough to flush off the heat in stomach, added flavors are usually stomach disrupters," Ramdin replies in a flow.

"But uncle, these institutes prepare students. I have also joined one institute and it has really turned my interface. Once, I used to be a super dumb student but now IIT entrance and other engineering exams seems chocolaty puddle to me," Boy intervenes in meanwhile.

Aditya throws a smile, and throws conclusive say, "Son, you are still too young, there is a world beyond the entrance havocs. You will learn soon…will tell you more if I get an opportunity to meet you again," Aditya pats him on shoulder, shakes hand with Ramdin and adds, "Ok, Ramdin brother, I'm leaving to computer shop for now. Will see you in the evening and yes send your kids to my house, I'll take care of them."

Aditya arranges a laptop, internet provider accessories with few much-needed household to get settled at a minimum needed scale.

The game was on. Everything had gained full gears; Aditya was now well settled in the new vicinity and space bargain. Gradually, Aditya had developed good relation with few people around. He normally used to talk petite but spent bulk lots of time at the tea stall and saloon. The owner of tea stall, Ramdin was now a very good pal of him. Aditya's time started getting shared with Bishmill and Misba, son and daughter respectively. He had decided to give free teaching to them.

Along with the teaching, he also begins up with article, phrase formation, which were supposed to be published in various tits-bits through many different media forms. ❑

28. Unknown reporter

Aditya had already preplanned the strategy to be applied, though he was not sure for its success. The tactic he made remained anonymous to all. While life kept breathing at the ventilators of adverse lifestyle. On the other hand, some very vigorous effervesce was all set to open the air tight bottle of black ill tradition, no one ever knew those fizz had little more thrust to invite dismantling cracks.

It was around six in the evening; still long enough for the Sun to dim down. Bishmill was sitting on sparsely left space on the floor, solving problems of calculus, while Aditya was busy reading some externals being leaned outside at the windowsill.

"Sir, can I opt for study in Design?" Bishmill's question popped in violating the unheard decibels. Aditya was bound to turn back, he stared sharp into Bishmill's eyes. His eyes turn wide, plasmatic trace resembling thread turns thicker and prominent. He moves towards the door.

"I'm sorry sir. I just..." Bishmill perceives of having committed a gaffe. But, almighty only knew what made Aditya react. Aditya leaps outside the main gate of premises, taking the road to *Gandhi Maidan*. The numbed man kept walking and walking waiting for the destination to come by. He always walks long in search of some omen to light when dark clouds overcast. So, many thoughts start gripping his thoughts, yet his feet keep traversing meters and meters.

"Son, please give me some alms in the name of Almighty. He will give you all success ahead. I have not eaten anything since last two days," someone softly screamed pulling corner of his *kurta*. He looks aside, towards bottom. An old man just managed to stand getting support of a stick. His spine almost seemed to be failed, while his eyes defined lots of experience. The skin of old man almost gave the impression of being completely hung over his weak calcium frames. The attire was similar to that of Sai Baba.

Though Aditya was an atheist, he believed on Sai Baba, and loved to help needy. There used to be a time when he was a big devotee and religious by nature. But the instance, decade of years back, had drawn away all related beliefs. That time he was under Internship at an Architectural firm at Bhubaneswar, and an important verdict was to be announced by The Honorable Supreme Court of India. The long awaited Ayodhya issue was to be solved, and all ways, lanes, public spaces were all vacant. The ghost riders were waiting for their feast, a vision was lightening within the skull of young aspiring Architect. Fortunately, tight administration was capable to trigger down any such chances, peace remained everywhere even after the verdict. A pleasing decision had come by; the land was to be equally distributed in three equal parts, one each for Hindu Temple, *Akhada* of RSS and one for the Muslim Mosque.

Ah...why to believe on that god, whose name is raged by the followers while butchering down other religion follower? How can that supposed to be 'Almighty' be the one if he can't secure the inhuman act at his name?

Aditya hands over a hundred rupees note to the saint, who looked like a beggar. The beggar feels delighted; he leaves from there floating away numerous blessings to Aditya. This incidence turned Aditya rethink about the issue, which Bishmill had asked, he rushes back to his place taking up an auto rickshaw.

When he reaches home, he sees Bishmill hanging at the road-facing window. Bishmill gets overjoyed watching him return back, he rushes downstairs to receive Aditya.

Bishmill says, "I'm sorry sir; I'll never repeat these talks agin. I never knew it will hurt you," Bishmill tries seeking an excuse, "Yesterday my teacher was talking about a leader, Aditya Sinha, who died in an accident few months back. You know he was a great Architect and Designer, his thoughts were vivid and par above natural thinking…"

Aditya intervenes in the middle, "and you know he was killed only for this mere reason, that he tried practicing at the best. Bishmill, this field is not safe if your vision is high, but don't worry someday the sun will again shine to full glory. The overcast will get over for sure."

"I didn't get you sir," says Bishmill.

Aditya smiles and adds stepping up to his habitable space, "Let it be Bishmill, we will talk some other time. Anyway, let's get upstairs to see how many problems have you solved correctly?"

"Ok Sir," Bishmill says and starts walking upstairs along with him.

***

Aditya had started living a multi faced life, a teacher in front of all around while a reporter after day falls. Almost, after a span of forty-five days that had passed by, the whole bill was fragmented into twelve different articles and an additional article dedicated to the overview of Naxalism.

Night was at full swing, the stars in the sky were well complementing the rays from the bright beautiful moon. Aditya was penning the articles in his notebook; the ongoing article was titled as number thirteen. Soon a wide smile appears on his face; he bolts his pen and rises up from the stands up. The last article was over through pen. Just in a while he opens up the flap of the laptop, makes a new folder titled 'Education Bill' and generates new MS Word file within it. He starts typing the penned article there. The job was getting articulated in the executable form.

Aditya takes another three days to type them all. He makes new facebook accounts, profiles and pages with the thought to promote his cause. He makes a personal profile with name, 'Adiraj Shrivastava' and a page and group with name, 'Education Reforms by Late Aditya Sinha'. Aditya was very decisive about the vision, and the goal was to be achieved by hook or crook.

How unpredictable life is? Aditya, a dedicated family lover and a social man, was now living the life of an unknown reporter staying in the world of unknowns. He had all communication sources, even had all the persons to communicate with still he was unable to merely greet even. Yet the fragileness was not longing on him, he was badly immersed into the river, which was to end up in the sea of perfection.

After the preparation of articles in electronic format, and

next was to find the perfect sources. He searches all known newspaper dailies and weekly socio political journals. After some thorough analysis, he observes an urgent need for various language translations including Hindi for the sake of global reach. Understanding the need for same, he finds various locally available various language translators. After a struggle of some around one week, he gets translators for nine Indian languages. Very soon the task of translation begins, which gets over by one more week.

Aditya starts sending the articles to various media sources including National news channels. The preparations for the big revolution were approaching a close.

The matter sent by Aditya becomes a great TRP increaser and competition factor for media. It becomes a sizzler for the Moment. Rest all happenings in country had lost their priority.

Unaware of the happenings in the media backdoor, Aditya kept anxiously waiting for the news to arrive. Finally, it was a day after five days. He pounces at the dragged in newspaper at the bottom of the door. He opens it up anxiously, and there it was, headline read in red bold fonts–The big cover up from the diary of Aditya Sinha. This moment was extremely blazing and celebratory for the hero behind it. He smiles wide and full, looks up towards the ceiling and closes his eyes. He very quickly wraps up the whole article and gets ready very soon. Enthusiasm was not letting his feet on the earth.

He sets out on the street, walking to find more of the newspaper to check for the viability of similar headlines. He keeps smiling within self out of excitement, which was making numerous people giggle on him. But, the crazy rebel keeps walking un-feared for any thing around.

He takes glance at all the newspapers available in the shop. All of them had covered up the similar story; the saga of jingoism had found its click.

With the preceding days, stories keeps finding place in some or other columns in all the media sources. Even news channels had started broadcasting the issue. Many news channels had begun a news show dedicated towards discussion on this matter.

Good things come late, but come for sure.

❑

29. Crossing the line

Our country has been suffering terrific by the blaze of fire in form of taunting Education System from long time. All the students, guardians have remained numb and underactive against same, that is but obviously expected from the crowd running behind the momentary happiness. The fog and frost of chill Gandhi honoring greenery have come out as biggest of barrier between wisdom and big bosses, administrators, educationalists and many as such. For the unique attribute of being cold and chilled, this fire never gave us an opportunity to project the consequence. Following which, we have become a Nation with maximum number of professionals, with least rate in efficient quality.

But some beautiful happenings were destined to happen; Saturn's eye was soon to fall upon self. The deeds by unknown reporter had spread brisk than fire. The silver point collection was now visible from behind the billows. The gallons of true happiness were to soon overlay *Aryavarta*.

Aditya was sleeping to sweetest of sleep, unaware of the resonating climate around. Some noise of mob ravished the beautiful sleep he was in, his eyes opened off in a while. He annoyingly looks on both the sides and then towards the ceiling and picks up his mobile phone. The digital clock acclaimed, sixth of a day remaining for the noon to arrive. He rises up and peeps through the small window.

A flood of heads was visible; the march seemed a promising and confident one. Aditya adjusts his spectacles, and now the banners and posters were sparsely visible to him. He assumed the visuals being halluciNation, thereby wiping the glass and even he doubted his ear. The young lads were walking tying red scarf against COACHING INSTITUTES.

He presses his bottom lip, removing the spectacles; runs thumb and its neighbor (finger) from inner corner of eyes to bottom of nose. Aditya bends his head facing the sky, while some precious emotion pearls find way through. Unknowingly stimulus responds, fingers get affirmed in a fist while hand, wrist draws an acute angle with biceps and lips too get in some pleasing action as he softly says, "Yes!" The Moment was over joyous for him. The kid of past seemed to have incurred in him. The job of unknown reporter had started paying back at best.

'*Jadi tor dak shune kyu na aashe, tumi ekla chalo re!*'

These lyrics meant a lot to Aditya as booster, he very often used to listen to this song when everything around seemed falling wrong and suffocating. And today, it is showing the significance too. His solely traversed distances seemed nearing destination.

He runs downstairs, to witness dream from close, in the just awoken state. He just puts on a blue cotton *kurta* anonymously well complementing white trouser he wore. He joins the march along with the young revolutionaries.

Young comrades were yelling best to their energy, as nothing else around could be heard. The agitation and firmness spoke of the resilient nature of the revolution.

Aditya bends aside, gets close to one of lad and asks, wearing a smile, "Do you think, it's going to be successful?"

"What uncle?" He asks.

Yes, the sound waves of revolution were more prevalent to let a talk occur. Aditya smiles more looking at the reaction, as it reflected jingoism level of the heads walking all along.

Aditya repeats the question getting closer to the lad's ear.

"Yes Uncle. It will be, it will be, we youth can't be befooled and made to walk on wrong path for long. History says, revolution always happen when wrong elements begin rising," boy replied in a loud tone. Aditya was just able to locate what boy said. He smiles again and pats on the boy's back. The boy again starts yelling the jingle of upheaval.

The sun was performing to full at the Patna Street, and the young rebels kept marching with full energy glooming parallel with sun's fierceness. Sense of ultimate satisfaction is clearly seen on Aditya's eyes.

***

It had started happening all around. Newspapers and news channels kept reporting me about the gigantic sedition that Nation was heading towards. It turned vigorous and spontaneous very soon.

Coaching institutes had started vacating; Nationwide rallies were being organized against their practice. But the good thing was an appeal made in the newspaper articles were widely accepted by the crowd. It was another movement marching ahead with the weapon of Non-Violence and Truth. It was a very overwhelming situation for whole Nation to witness philosophy of the Gujarati gentleman applied by the young blood, who are often disguised to be oozing and eruptive.

Youth started following the path of non-cooperation in the movement, with demand to enforce Aditya's education bill.

Students started boycotting classes; many colleges witnessed null attendance during examination. It didn't remain confined to small concerns, students of more than fifty colleges from India refused to take degree from university.

The revolution starts getting support from all corners and agencies, even many School-Teachers, College Professors and few Educationalists start organizing rallies asking government to enforce bill at an earliest.

The color didn't leave land beyond borders even; students studying in foreign countries started raising voice against Indian Government. Soon matter reached beyond the demand for bill, public started asking for reopening the file of Aditya's death. Whole Nation was now suspecting it to be a murder instead of an accident.

Whole Nation was now together seeking justice for all. The final destination of Aditya started seeming very close and touchable. Whole country starts making their presence on the streets and roads. Professionals from all walks, students and teachers all come up together with a sole aim of bill's enforcement with reopening of Aditya's case.

Froth start ramping through the government's bench. Death always calls one nearer to imprudent deeds. They start trying to shut down the non-violent, non-cooperation through force and violence.

Political Leaders wear Gandhi caps not in respect and not because they follow him but to mask all what Bapu hated most.

Government tries controlling the uprising through all means they could. Police makes blows to the activists, many mothers' lad get injured and fractured, but none of them take charge against *Gandhian* philosophy. This step by government acts as fuel for the fire, movement turns fiercer by flame and darker by shade.

Public doesn't leave the premises of the Parliament as well, rallies also begin happening in front of the big house. Media TRP issue keeps acting as a catalyst. All sources try heaping at best to receive the maximum they could.

Days passed, weeks passed, so do month, none of them dragged a step back. Government remains foolishly standing, affirm to their thought, nor the upheaval found any bolting or pause.

The uprising results in many losses to Nation's economy, development and progress finds the state of statics.

Expectation seemed swaying by the side of revolution. Aditya starts turning happily impatient, the act by Nation becomes the reason for his happiness while elongation of result starts adding to his distress.

Mixed emotions rust one most.

❑

30. Bright morning

Sun had already left reddish hue back. Bright gloom was all the way to begin a new twenty fours. Shining pearl glitters and sparkles deep at the curvature of fallen indigo writing juice, while the pen remained uncapped, lying on the snowy papyrus, few penning was clearly visible. The cholera carrier came buzzing near his respiratory opening finally landing on his ear. Aditya's eyes opened in a shudder, he never knew how precious the day was to be. He rises from the bed; the carpet of vivid sunray was already spread on sparsely seen floor finish, while rest remained occupied with so many newspapers, books, notes, drawing sheets and many other stationary articles. His feet yanks towards the balmy mat, he marches five steps forward to reach the teak table, he reaches out to pick spectacles. Putting it on, he looks around; newspaper was partially pushed in through the thin opening below the door. He bends down to fetch it; he places it on table and gets into the washroom. After coming back to living space, he picks up the small encompassed replica reflector, his beard lied in same line with neck ball and the hair was even below that. Few dark circles were partially noticeable on his brownish complexion. Accept his appearance nothing else was paying back for the firm work done.

Disappointment had become regular custom of his life since long; he walks out on the street towards 'Hanuman Temple', it was not the temple which attracted him follow a daily custom as such. The panorama was subtle intermingling of adverse culture and tradition, a perfect landscaping where the bells of temple chromed exactly when the priest used to deliver 'Aazaan' in adjacent mosque, the harmony was perfect indeed.

He reaches the regular stall, where he used to take morning tea. "Today you are little late sir," said the stall keeper. Aditya had developed a very sound relation with all people around in the days spent around.

"Yes, I was reading till very late last night, and some other works were being done too, Ramdin. How are you and how your kids are doing?" delivered Aditya.

"Everything running super and perfect sir, even Bishmill and Misba are doing well. Bishmill is almost sure about getting through engineering entrance this time. Things have changed a lot after your intervention," Ramdin explained.

"Nothing as such Ram. It is merely the consequence of your goodness and the labor, they are doing. Blessings work for noble men and it is happening here as well," Aditya said, meanwhile, Aditya's vision interlaced with a crowd of young men at the corner. Numerous expressions were bursting within the murmuring noise they made.

Aditya moved towards them, holding the glass of tea. "It is really unbelievable, how government can be so subtle and sublime?" said one of those from crowd.

"Yes mate, but all credit goes to Aditya Sinha. How happy would he have been watching his dream coming to reality? He really proved out to be changer being the change," said another guy folding back the newspaper. A lots of crowd was also collected in the saloon nearby, they were tucked watching news broadcasting some live reactions. The colors of happiness and delight had overcastted all momentary pains and hurts among the youth seen.

"What a pure soul Aditya Sinha is? God never lets good people stay long. His leadership will be missed in the impending days to come by," two college-going girls chatted while rolling down their bicycles. Aditya could not at all collect the happenings around, though one thing had become very transparent and almost understood to him. Some major occurrence had dropped in which had in any way connection with him. It was after long, he was hearing his own name being chanted around for some goodness.

Aditya dashed back to Ramdin, "Arre, Ramdin! What has happened? Why are all talking so much about Late Parliamentarian Aditya today?"

"Oh, sir! Didn't you read today's newspaper? Long after

the government has decided to implement some bill, which had some relations with Aditya Babu," said Ramdin.

"Oh my god!" tears started flowing through; he was taken aback by extreme happiness and aghast. But Ramdin could never know the buried emotion and cloud of success rains within his abdomen. He started jogging away from there, care freely without considering the arounds including the traffic. "Sir… sir…" Ramdin kept calling, but something anonymous was yanking. The Kolhapuri footwear, he wore was putting many imprints both on him and the Patna Station road. His feet got it's skin peeled, making little plasma flow appear, while the impulse between his slipper and road was bringing knocking sound, though none was never to be known by the breathers around.

The tanned *kurta* he wore showed its extreme affect as sweat was thickly ornamented on his skin. He ran to the upper floor, where he lived. He opened the television and jabbed newspaper as well, all was turning in a rush. Aditya was a true resemblance of a kid unpacking his gift anticipating best of the toys within.

Aditya's predictions came true and candid, but the projections in his small television screen felt as biggest as of mountain.

"It has almost been six months when Adi left us all alone. It is really a matter of great pride and pleasure, that his dream is coming true on the day auspicious date of his birth. He has really set an example for the youth of today by perfectly defining what a leader is."

"Today it's his birthday, do you have to say something on it?" asked the correspondent.

"It was really a substance of pinnacled grief for some time around. But great legendary book 'Geeta' says something, what again keeps me strong. Soul never dies. In whichever world he may be, this precious gift of occasion would be not letting his feet on ground. I'm very proud to be his soul mate, who indeed is an idol for generations of present time and those to come by, Aditya never dies…" Emotions were being moistened and dampened.

"So this was the live coverage from the home of Aditya Sinha, the rebel leader, who died in an accident six months ago. And today we have his bill finally passed under state of observation. The whole Nation is celebrating the big change today, but unfortunately the lamps of delight can't be lit in home of change behind change."

Aditya's visionary sphere was in a fix, the liquid of emotion came on its way. The planets were on their role, the irony of situation was playing the fastest inning of years. He removes his spectacles, wiping the rolling liquid, his eyes stuck to the bold letters of 'The Times of India', long after he was reading, the grey color painted by expectation had outreached him.

Aditya drops down on his knees. The two sayings came very true, the fruits of seeds sown were upfront, "When you want something, the universe conspires in helping you to achieving it," and "Universe runs on the law of gravitation, it depends if one is prone to accentuation of black or white." All came perfect; the dream, seen many years ago, was finally blown through the mould.

He was unable to realize, if it was a moment of happiness, cheers and celebration or instant of deep thronged pain.

The change seemed broken and shattered. After long the workstation was oozed with unwanted climate called life settlement churner, while the winter of revolution was forcing new clothing and overlaying. He was flop to conclude, he wanted to hug Trisha, Kartik, Mom and Dad but…this was badly fit into his cerebrum that–these revolution are merely an outcome of, he being declared dead. To Aditya, the certificate of 'No more' was indeed catalyst for the much-needed bill to be passed. Was it the pull of *Shaitan* or love, the power of accentuation was making his thoughts fragile, unmoved.

A man who never let any irony overcast his brightness was getting crapped in puddle of dilemma.

The dreams, which were stationed on my eyes,
Becoming frost, they have gone beyond my eyes.
You and I were sitting beneath the shade of those beautiful dreams,
Where are we moving leaving those dreams?
It is end of a story or some other yet to begin;
It's a new morning or night is yet to begin?

www.ingramcontent.com/pod-product-compliance
Ingram Content Group UK Ltd.
Pitfield, Milton Keynes, MK11 3LW, UK
UKHW021700190726
13853UKWH00001B/379